Chapter 1

A Scot Is Born

The story begins. Wallace Alan Leslie was born on August 23, 1888, in Auchleven, Scotland, a village near Aberdeenshire. Wallace's father's name was Joshua, and his mom was Catherine, whom everyone called Kate.

Joshua was a wood craftsman; he was known all over Northern Scotland for his fine craftsmanship in wood furniture, and he also had a large herd of sheep. Kate was a homemaker and seamstress. The Leslies owned a stone cottage that was used for their dwelling. Joshua's workshop was attached to the back of the cottage. The sheep corral behind the workshop was a rock-structure-type barn built into the hillside. The roof was overlaid with logs and slate rock covered in sod; this kept the sheep sheltered and warm in the winter.

During this time, in Scottish history, a family produced all of their own foods. Clothing needs were bartered or sold. What produce and crafts they were able to produce, they used to barter, eat, and prosper. The village of Auchleven was a close-knit village with most of the residents having the last name of Leslie. The Leslie clan and family were one of the larger clans in Northeastern Scotland at this time.

Wallace was the fourth child to be born to Joshua and Kate. He had one older brother, Samuel, and two older sisters, Ruth and Ester.

As Wallace grew in years, his dad started giving him more responsibilities. One of his duties was to help take care of the sheep.

He would help his older brother Samuel drive the sheep to and from the high meadow and take care of newborn lambs. This taught him to be an outdoorsman and to love and appreciate life and nature. He would help his dad slaughter a lamb sometimes for food, which taught him the importance of life and the taking of life so he and his family would have food.

He would work with his dad in his woodshop, and he learned how to turn a plain piece of wood into a beautiful work of art and craftsmanship.

Wallace was a highly intelligent child, and his local schoolmaster told Joshua and Kate that Wallace needed more advanced studying and school. To challenge him, the schoolmaster suggested Edinburgh. Joshua and Kate discussed sending Wallace to a school in Edinburgh for gifted students but were hesitant because of the cost and also of Wallace's age. At that time, he was only twelve years old. Joshua suggested that he would write his cousin, Edwin Leslie, who had a large estate in Caledon, Ireland, and ask if Wallace could come and stay with him. That way, Wallace could study at St. Macartan's school of higher learning. Kate agreed that the local school was not challenging Wallace, and a child with his abilities should not be held back.

Several weeks later, Joshua received a letter from his cousin Edwin, saying he would be honored to have Wallace come to stay with him while he was doing his studies at St. Macartan.

When Joshua and Kate told Wallace that they wanted him to go stay with his cousins in Ireland, Wallace was terribly upset. But he knew deep down inside this was what he needed to do. He was totally bored at his local school and knew much more than his teacher. He had never met his cousins but had seen pictures of them and their large estate. He had always dreamed of riding a horse; now, he would be living where they had a large horse barn with many horses.

The following Monday, Joshua and Kate took Wallace to the train station in Aberdeen to begin his trip to Caledon, Ireland. This was the first time Wallace had ever gone anywhere without his parents. He had traveled to Edinburgh once with his dad but had never traveled without his family.

Kate's aunt was supposed to meet Wallace at the train depot in Edinburgh and help him get on the correct train going to Ayr, Scotland. When Wallace reached the station at Edinburgh, it was dark, and he did not know anyone and did not see his aunt. He had never felt so lost in his life. Everyone was busy getting on other trains. The train attendants were loading luggage into horse-drawn carriages. Everyone was moving at a fast pace, and Wallace was scared and confused. He then saw a train attendant helping passengers with their transfers, so he started to walk over and ask him for help. Then, a young man grabbed his little canvas bag with his clothes, personal belongings, his train ticket, and his money and ran into the darkness. Luckily, the train attendant saw the thief and chased after him. Wallace just stood there frozen in panic. His parents had trusted him to travel alone, and the first time he got out of sight, he screwed everything up. He started to feel sick at his stomach, tears started to flow. Suddenly, he heard a familiar voice, his Aunt Ruth! She said, "Wallace, are you okay? What is wrong, I have looked everywhere for you. Where is your bag?"

He started to cry, and he said, "I can't do anything right. My parents trusted me to travel alone, and now, I have lost my money, my ticket, my clothes, and everything."

A man touched Aunt Ruth's arm. "Excuse me, ma'am!" It was the train attendant who explained to Aunt Ruth that he had seen the thief grabbed the boy's bag and ran. He was not able to catch him and get the bag back. Wallace told the attendant it had all his tickets in it: the ticket from Edinburgh to Ayr, his ship passage ticket from Ayr to Dublin, and his ticket from Dublin to Glaslough. It also had his clothes and the money his parents had given him.

The train attendant said, "This happens way too often. It is one of the homeless kids that lived on the street here in Edinburg that stole your bag." He added, "Come with me, and I will issue you brand new tickets." Wallace was able to get new tickets and still had time to catch the train. Aunt Ruth gave him all the money she had on her. He was off again, but now, he had no clothes and not enough money to buy any.

The plan was that one of his father's friends, William Carter, who lived in Ayr would meet him at the train and help Wallace get on the right ship sailing to Dublin. When Wallace arrived, William Carter was standing outside the train depot holding a pole with Wallace's name on the banner. As soon as Wallace departed the train, he saw Mr. Carter. He wished that the last stop had been as easy. He explained what had happened at the last train stop. Mr. Carter said, "That's no problem, Wallace. We will take care of everything tomorrow. You are not supposed to catch the ship till the day after tomorrow, so we will have time to get new clothes and get you ready to go."

Mr. Carter was a really nice man. Wallace finally felt like everything was going to be okay. After a good breakfast, Mrs. Carter took Wallace down to the clothing store and purchased a new bag and some new clothes. Wallace said, "I don't know how I will ever be able to repay you."

Mr. Carter said, "Your dad has been so kind to me over the years, so maybe this is a way I can repay him."

The following morning, Mr. Carter took Wallace to the harbor and helped him get on the right ship. Mr. Carter told Wallace that his cousin, Edwin Leslie, would have someone to meet him at the Dublin Harbor and would ride with him for the rest of the way by train to Glaslough in Ireland.

Wallace had been on the ship for about one hour when seasickness set in. He had planned to stay on the upper deck during the crossing but ended up in his bed the whole time. He was not able to eat anything during the whole trip.

When the ship reached Dublin Harbor, a young man, Sean McClain, was waiting for him. Sean worked for Edwin Leslie. Sean and Wallace hit it off right away. Sean had grown up on the Leslie Estate, and he told Wallace, "You are going to love it there."

When they arrived, Wallace could not believe his eyes. He had never seen a house this large and nice, not even in Edinburgh. They were greeted by a butler named Samuel. He told the boys to go and bathe in the guest quarters, and he would prepare some clothes for them, which were suitable for dining. After a good bath, Wallace and Sean dressed and were escorted to the dining room where Edwin and Catherine Leslie were waiting on them.

After one of the best meals Wallace had ever eaten, he was questioned by his cousins. They showed him his room and told him that their home was his home during the time he would be living with them and going to school in Ireland.

The next day, Sean met Wallace after breakfast. They went down to the stables and saddled two horses. Wallace had ridden before but was not the horseman that Sean was. Sean gave Wallace a tour of the estate. Wallace could not believe how his cousins lived. He had never met anyone who lived on an estate with servants and all the amenities of the estate.

Edwin and Catherine were very nice and treated Wallace like he was their own son. The following Monday, Wallace started school at St. Macartan. This school was quite different from his school like night and day. St. Macartan was a very structured school—most of the students were gifted students of financial status. Some of the best teachers in Ireland taught there. Wallace really had to apply himself, but he liked the challenge. His cousins, Edwin and Catherine, encouraged him and supported Wallace in every way possible with his studies. The estate had a large study with hundreds of books. Wallace would spend hours in the study reading and preparing for school.

In several years, when Wallace graduated, he was at the top of his class. He applied at the university back in Edinburgh, Scotland, and was accepted there to continue his studies.

It was time for him to leave his cousins, Edwin and Catherine. They had been like parents to him, giving him more than he could ever repay them for a good education, home, and a great loving family. It was so hard to leave these great people that had given so much and only asked Wallace to love them like parents. As Wallace was getting ready to leave for Edinburgh, Edwin told Wallace to always strive to be a better person each day and to help anyone who he might meet in life and that was in need, no matter their skin color, class status, or financial status. He said, "We are all children of God, and it is our responsibility to help our brothers and sisters here on earth."

Edwin handed Wallace an envelope as he boarded the train. He said, "Read this once you are on the train. Take pride in your name, but remember, always help those who are less fortunate."

When Wallace got seated on the train and opened the envelope and read the letter, it said:

> Wallace, you have been such a blessing to Catherine and me, you are the son we never had. We will always love you, and you are always welcome in our home. We know you will succeed in whatever endeavor you pursue. You are a special young man. Wallace, a little history lesson about your name. Always honor, respect, and uphold the Leslie name. We have traced the Leslie name and ancestry back to Attila the Hun. The first Leslie came from and was a Hungarian nobleman called Bartholomew Leslie. He was the chamberlain and protector of Margaret, Queen of Scotland. The family motto Grip Fast originated from him while fleeing enemies. Queen Margaret fell off her horse in a river. Bartholomew held his hand out and said, "Hold on or grip fast. He pulled her onto the back of his horse's saddle and escaped the enemy, saving the queen. In thanks for saving the queen, King James IV told Bartholomew to start at the castle gate and ride north until his horse tires, and he would grant him the land. Bartholomew does as the king has ordered and rode his horse north until the horse

tires. When he stopped, he told a villager, "I declare this land, Leslie."

Wallace said to himself, *I have heard of the story, but not this detailed.* He was proud of his name but mostly proud of the family he knew and loved.

Wallace arrived at Edinburgh University, one of the top universities in Europe. Wallace is a polished young student, well-read, and educated from St. Macartan's in Ireland. Edwin and Catherine have had a positive influence on Wallace, and he fits in well at the university.

Wallace decided to pursue a degree as a geologist, specializing in petroleum research. Wallace believed that the future of the industrial growth of Europe would be powered by petroleum. Wallace began his college studies; he loved geology and excelled in his classes. His professors took him and the other students on field trips, and they were able to experience hands-on training in their studies. Petroleum production was just now starting to excel around the world, and Wallace knew he had picked the perfect field to be in at this time in history.

Chapter 2

Wallace's First Love

One of Wallace's professors asked Wallace if he would like to go on an expedition with one of Scotland's top geologists to the northern coast of Scotland. Wallace said yes; he was so excited to actually be in the presence of a great geologist like Dr. Robert Dunn. When Wallace arrived at the drill site in Northern Scotland, he was greeted by Dr. Dunn and his daughter McKenzie. When Wallace and McKenzie's eyes made contact, they both were so captivated with each other; they couldn't stop staring or take their eyes off each other. Wallace had girlfriends before, but he had never been so mesmerized by any woman in his life. Her beauty dwarfed even the beauty of the goddess Nefertiti. She was close to six feet tall with long black hair, blue eyes, and olive skin. She also seemed infatuated with Wallace. Wallace finally realized that Dr. Dunn was trying to speak to him. He apologized for his rudeness of staring. Dr. Dunn said, "I thought maybe you had met McKenzie before, the way you two were staring at each other."

"No, sir, I apologize. I was caught off guard by the absolute beauty of your daughter."

Dr. Dunn said, "Thank goodness, she takes after her mom and not me. I had the same response as you did the first time, I laid eyes on McKenzie's mom."

Wallace helped Dr. Dunn for two weeks on the study; that he was doing at the oil shale rock site in Thurso on the north coast of

Scotland. McKenzie had just graduated from Edinburgh University and was working on her doctoral degree with her father, Dr. Dunn, in Geology. The two weeks that Wallace got to spend with McKenzie and her father were the two best weeks of his life. McKenzie and Wallace were both infatuated and physically attracted to each other. Plus, when it came to discussing geology, they both had a desire to share their knowledge with others. They sat for hours just staring at each other and talking about their childhoods and the dreams of their futures.

McKenzie told Wallace about a cave she had discovered on the coast near the drilling site where they were doing their research. She asked Wallace if he would like to explore it with her. Wallace said yes. He was so excited to be able to do something fun with McKenzie where they could be alone together without the stares of some of the other researchers. McKenzie told Wallace to meet her outside the cottage the following morning where she and her father were staying. She said that she would bring a picnic lunch and a bottle of wine. She told Wallace to bring a rope in case they needed it to get down into the deeper parts of the cave. Wallace was so excited that he couldn't sleep, and so is McKenzie. Ever since the day both of them met for the first time, both of them had a hidden desire to hold each other in a passionate embrace. McKenzie was an incredibly beautiful woman and had many boyfriends, but there was something about Wallace; she had a desire to hold him so close and to never let him go. It was almost like she had an intuition that Wallace would be her lover, mate, and husband the rest of her life. She tried to think of a day when she would not love or hold him in a long passionate embrace, but she couldn't. She knew, without a doubt, that she loved this man and this man only, and he would be her husband the rest of her life.

That night, McKenzie dreamed about Wallace; they were all alone in her dream, and he pulled her close to himself and kissed her neck. His hand caressed her breast and slowly moved down to her leg. She was breathing so hard. She awaked herself. She wrapped her arms around her pillow, and pulled it to her breast and said, "I'm so in love with you, Wallace Leslie. I want to spend the rest of my life with you".

The next morning, Wallace was at McKenzie's cottage shortly after daybreak. She welcomed him in, and he gave her a little kiss on the forehead and said, "Good morning, beautiful angel." She desired to pull him close and kiss his lips, but she played it cool and said, "I will have lunch ready in a few minutes."

Dr. Dunn walked in, and Wallace greeted him, "Good Morning Dr. Dunn."

He responded, "Good morning to you, Wallace. McKenzie told me you are going to explore the cave down next to the ocean, you two please be safe and watch for the rising tide. While you are at the cave, if you see any oil shale rocks, collect some for me."

Wallace responded, "We will be careful, and I will bring you some shale rocks back if I see any."

McKenzie walked back into the room with a small rucksack. She said, "Wallace, here is our lunch. Do you mind carrying it?"

Wallace said, "No, I don't mind, I have the rope, and I brought two walking sticks to help us navigate through the boulders field."

Dr. Dunn said, "Be safe and have fun."

Wallace and McKenzie began their hike to the cave. Once they were out of sight of the cottage, McKenzie reached over and took Wallace's hand. She pulled him close and kissed him passionately on the lips. Wallace put his arms around her, and they kissed for several minutes. McKenzie said, "I have wanted to do that from the very first time I saw you a couple of days ago."

Wallace said, "I have wanted to kiss you so much but did not want you to think I was a savage."

McKenzie responded by kissing him again and said, "Kiss me, you, savage."

Wallace and McKenzie made their way down to the cave. Wallace said, "We will have to leave before 3:00 p.m. this afternoon because the cave will start to fill with water from the evening tide."

When they reached the cave, McKenzie handed Wallace the lantern she had brought with her. Wallace lit the lantern, and they began their journey back into the depths of the cave; they had gone about a hundred feet when the cave passage opened up into a large cavern. There was broken pottery and glass on the floor. There was a bench and a bed that had been hewed into the rock. Wallace said, "I bet someone has used this cave as a hideout in the past. However, I would not want to get trapped in here when the tide starts to rise. If you did not know the layout of the cave, it could be fatal."

McKenzie said, "Look here, Wallace, this looks like prime oil shale rock. Let's do an experiment!" McKenzie crushed the shale rock with another rock then took a piece of paper and lit it from the lantern. She then laid the paper on the oil shale rock, and it began to burn. She said, "This is what my dad has been looking for, let's collect some to take back to him."

After exploring for a couple of more hours, McKenzie and Wallace made it back to the entrance of the cave. McKenzie pulled out a tablecloth and spread it on a large rock and laid out the food and wine she had brought for their picnic. Wallace positioned two large stones for them to sit on. Wallace blessed the food, and they began their meal.

McKenzie said, "This may be inappropriate," but she asked Wallace, "how do you feel about me?"

Wallace said, "I am crazy about you. I cannot get you off my mind night and day. I hope, someday, if you feel the same way as I do, maybe you would be my wife, McKenzie. I have never felt for anyone what I feel for you. Every time I look at you or hear your voice, my heart beats fast, I have all these funny feelings all over my body."

McKenzie responded, "Wallace, I feel the same way. I want to spend the rest of my life with you. I want to hold you close all night long. I want to make love to you every day for the rest of my life." McKenzie added, "I apologize, I just let my emotions get away from me."

Wallace responded, "McKenzie, I feel the same way. I can't imagine living one day of my life without you."

McKenzie said, "I have always been a very independent person, even from my childhood into womanhood. If I want to do something, I do it with no regrets. I hope what I'm about to say does not cause you to lose respect for me, and I hope it does not cause you to love me any less than what you do now. Wallace, I want to hold you, and I want you to make love to me. I have never been intimate with another man before in my life, but, Wallace, I want to be yours, and you'll be mine. I promise I will always be yours, and I want you to promise you will always be mine and only mine.

Wallace said, "It's not my nature to be so passionately drawn to anyone like I'm drawn to you, and I promise, I will always be your one and only love."

McKenzie cleaned the remaining food off the tablecloth. She slowly unbuttoned her dress and laid it to the side. She took Wallace's hand and gently pulled him to her, kissing his lips. Wallace's hand glided over McKenzie's soft body, caressing her breast, and his hand touched the warm curve of her back. McKenzie slowly unbuttoned Wallace's shirt and pants, and she gently pulled him next to her and leaned back onto the cloth. He kissed her neck; the sweet-salty taste of her skin was tantalizing. She pulled him so close; they were as one. They held each other and kissed for hours.

Wallace was awakened by a mist of seawater spraying on his back. He said, "McKenzie, the tide is coming in." Wallace and McKenzie scrambled to gather their clothes and rucksack and quickly exit the cave through knee-deep water.

Wallace pulled McKenzie to him and said, "McKenzie, I love you, and this has been the best day of my life. Will you marry me?"

McKenzie said, "Yes, Wallace Leslie, I will marry you, I will marry you, I will marry you!"

When they reached the cottage, Dr. Dunn was waiting on them. He said, "You two made the day of it."

McKenzie said, "Dad, I think we have found what you have been looking for," and pulled some of the oil shales from the rucksack.

Dr. Dunn responded, "This is prime oil shale rock."

"Dad, we found a whole mountain of it."

Dr. Dunn grabbed McKenzie, and they danced around the room. Dr. Dunn said, "I want to go back tomorrow with you two, and I want you to show me where you found the oil shale rock."

McKenzie said, "You two, guys, wash up, and I will fix us some dinner. I put a roast on to cook before we went exploring the cave today."

Dr. Dunn said, "Wallace, I have never seen McKenzie this happy before in her life, son. McKenzie really does like you, and I'm becoming quite fond of you too. Wallace, what are your feelings toward my daughter?"

Wallace responded, "Sir, they are all honorable, and I love your daughter very much. She is a special woman.

Dr. Dunn said, "Yes, she is."

After a fine dinner and glass of red Scottish wine, Dr. Dunn said, "We need to turn in early tonight, I want to go explore that cave first thing in the morning."

Wallace said, "Sir, I will head down to my cottage next door."

McKenzie said, "I will walk you to the door." As Wallace was getting ready to walk out the door, McKenzie whispered into his ear, "Don't lock your door, I will slip down to your cottage as soon as Dad goes to sleep." Wallace ran as fast as he could to his cottage and started cleaning up his room. He took a quick bath and lit some candles. He took some spice water that he had brought from his barber and sprinkled it on his face and under his arms. Wallace was so excited that he could feel his heart beating in his chest. Up until today, Wallace had never been with a woman, now, he was going to get to make love to the woman of his dreams two times in one day. Wallace's life had changed forever; he was getting ready to start a new adventure with the woman he had always dreamed of.

He heard McKenzie peck on the window! He ran so fast to the door that he tripped over a chair and crashed into the table. She came in and said, "Are you okay?"

He said, "Yes, I'm just so excited you are here."

McKenzie said, "I can't stay long, but I just had to hold you and kiss you one more time today."

Wallace said, "You better get used to it because my plan is to make love to you every day for the rest of my life." McKenzie took Wallace's hand and pulled him to his bed where she pushed him down on the bed and straddled him, holding his arms above his head while she kissed his neck and lips. After Wallace and McKenzie made love, Wallace fell asleep, and when he woke up, McKenzie was gone.

He looked at the clock, and it's just one hour before he was to meet with Dr. Dunn, so he got up and got ready to explore the cave again.

When Wallace arrived at Dr. Dunn's cottage, McKenzie already had breakfast sitting on the table. She said, "I'm glad you decided to have breakfast with us this morning, sleepyhead. Dr. Dunn said, "Did you sleep well, Wallace?"

Wallace responded, "I didn't get much sleep last night, but what sleep I got was the best I have ever had."

Dr. Dunn, Wallace, and McKenzie made it down to the cave. Dr. Dunn was amazed at the amount and quality of the oil shale rock vein that ran under the mountain. Dr. Dunn said, "You two have found what I've been looking for. We will start mining and drilling here as soon as we can get the crews moved up here."

That night after dinner, Wallace asked Dr. Dunn for McKenzie's hand in marriage. Dr. Dunn said, "Both of you have my blessings. I knew from that first day when you two met and could not take your eyes off each other, that both of you had found their true love that only comes, maybe, one time in a person's life. Wallace, you are a great young man, and it will be an honor to have you as a son-in-law. I want you to know, I will help you and McKenzie anyway I can in getting your careers off to a good start."

Two months later, Wallace graduated from Edinburgh University with a degree in geophysical engineering. Wallace and McKenzie were married and spent their honeymoon at his Uncle Edwin and Catherine's estate in Ireland. Shortly after Wallace's graduation, he was approached by a German oil company looking for a geologist.

Chapter 3

African Expedition

The company was the Leuna Oil Company. The vice president of the company met with Wallace and McKenzie when he found out that Wallace and McKenzie were both geologists. He said, "I must hire both of you. I will be getting two geologists for the price of one." Then he said, "I'm just joking." He said any expenses or services that Mrs. Leslie contributes to my company, she would be paid well for. Wallace and McKenzie discussed the job offer, which included all travel expenses and a large bonus for any oil reserve that they might discover.

Wallace and McKenzie agreed; this was what they had worked for and had dreamed of for many years. They met with Mr. Klaus, the vice president of Leuna Oil, and accepted his offer. Mr. Klaus told them that their first assignment would be going to a potential oil reserve in German East Africa. McKenzie asked Mr. Klaus if her father Dr. Dunn, a world-renowned geologist, could go with her and Wallace on this expedition. Mr. Klaus said, "Sure, it would be an honor to have a man with Dr. Dunn's credentials on this expedition."

Mr. Klaus informed Wallace and McKenzie that the German ship that will be taking them to the Port of Dar es Salaam will be leaving in a week. They both met with their local physician and were given medicine and advice about traveling in East Africa.

June 6, 1913, Wallace, McKenzie, and Dr. Dunn began their journey to German East Africa. They passed through the Suez Canal and down the East Coast of Africa to the port city of Dar es Salaam. There they boarded a train to the town of Moshi where they were met by German soldiers. Wallace and Dr. Dunn loaded all their supplies onto three Mercedes Benz trucks and started their adventure to the fabled giant volcano crater of Ngorongoro, which covers a landmass of 260 square miles and is two thousand feet deep. Two German farmers had found some raw crude oil bubbling out of the ground near the crater close to the coffee plantation called Endulen.

As the caravan moved slowly through the open savanna headed north, their first stop would be Arusha, then they would travel onto Ngorongoro Crater and then onto the coffee plantation at Endulen. As they traveled north, they saw vast herds of wildebeest and zebra grazing but always on the move. They saw herds of giraffes, elephants, and antelopes.

Wallace had read several books about Africa and saw pictures when he was at the university, but nothing could have prepared him for this vista of God's creation before mankind had destroyed most of the wildlife on this planet. McKenzie, her dad, and Wallace were mesmerized by the vast herds of animals. Occasionally, they would see a pride of lions sleeping or devouring a freshly killed meal. They arrived at the army base near Arusha just before sunset. McKenzie and Wallace both said at the same time, "That's the most beautiful sunset that we had ever witnessed." The sun looked so large as it was touching the earth and sky with acacia trees dotting the savanna. It was one of the most picturesque settings they have ever seen. It was like McKenzie and Wallace had been transported to another planet or another world; they definitely were not in Scotland anymore.

From the very first couple of miles that McKenzie and Wallace traveled, once they left Moshi, they both knew that they wanted to make Africa their home someday.

They were greeted by a German captain; he showed them to their quarters for the night. He said that the locals had prepared a feast for them, and he asked them if they would dine with him. As they dined, Wallace noticed the captain staring at McKenzie. He had gotten used to that by now because wherever they went, men were always captivated by her natural beauty. McKenzie did not ever act like she noticed men staring, yet he knew she had to. McKenzie never wore makeup; she always let her hair hang loose or pull it back into a ponytail. She often wore a hat or a beret with her dark-olive skin; there was no need for makeup. After a good dinner, they were entertained by the local African dancers.

That night, Wallace slept well and dreamed of living here in God's creation someday. They rose early the next morning, had breakfast, and headed north to the Ngorongoro Crater. They traveled all day and only saw a few people, a group of African Maasai, in full war bonnet headdress running across the African savanna with their spear in hand. The driver said, "If you don't bother them, they don't bother you. They are strange but really brave people." He said,

"Before a boy can become a man, he has to kill a lion with a spear." He said some of them ended up being the lion's dinner.

Late that afternoon, they stopped beside a river and set up camp. The African men riding in one of the trucks started immediately cutting thorn bushes and started building a thorn fence around their camp. Wallace asked the driver, "Why are they building a thorn fence around the camp."

And he said, "To keep the big cats and hyenas from eating us tonight." The driver suggested that they sleep in the back of the truck tonight; it will be a lot safer.

He said, "we will keep guards posted all night, but it is not unusual for a big cat to come into camp at night and drag someone away before anyone has time to react."

McKenzie and Wallace did not get any sleep that night. The jungle was alive, you could hear lions grunting, and occasionally, one will roar. Hyenas' cries send chills up your spine. The next morning, Wallace asked the driver, "How did you sleep?"

He said, "Like a baby. You will get used to it in a couple of nights." The next night, they did sleep like babies. They had fallen in love with Africa, and they never would go back to Europe if they didn't have to.

The next day, they passed a large river that had crocodiles in it that were over sixteen feet long, and the driver told them they weigh close to a ton. There were millions of pink flamingos, large groups of ostriches, and pools of hippopotamuses. The driver told them more native Africans were killed by hippopotamuses and crocodiles than they were killed by lions and leopards.

They finally reach the Ngorongoro Crater; they couldn't believe their eyes. The crater was so huge that it had its own ecosystem living within the crater. It was like seeing the world that time had forgotten, described in Edgar Rice Burroughs's book.

The trucks pulled into a farm owned by Hans and Otto Meyer, and they were greeted by some servants from the main house. Their driver told them, "We will stay here overnight then drive on to Endulen tomorrow." That night, they had dinner with Hans Meyers. He said his brother had taken some friends out on a hunting safari. He told them that he and Otto had started farming in the crater in 1899. He said it was a constant battle with local tribes, and the wildebeests which would destroy the crops, and the lions and leopards were always killing their livestock. He asked McKenzie if they would be interested in buying him out. They told him they loved it here, but they were just starting out in life, and they really had little money to buy land with. He said, "I will make you a deal you can't refuse."

Wallace asked Hans about the large mounds at the base of the crater that they saw as they were entering the farm. He said he really did not know, but he had been told by the locals that the ancient people that used to live in the crater used to bury their dead there and pile large rocks onto the graves. The next morning, as they started to leave, they thanked Hans for his hospitality. As they drove away, he said, "If you change your mind, this will make a great farm for you and your wife."

They reached Endulen just before sundown. They were met by the owners of the coffee plantation, Karl and Anna Muller. They were nice people, and they were so glad to have some European visitors. They told them they lived so far out that they never got any visitors. They showed them to their cottage. They had two small guest cottages for anyone visiting the area. The next morning, they awoke to the wonderful aroma of freshly brewed coffee and bacon, eggs, biscuits, and white gravy. It was heaven on earth. They dined outside under a veranda covered with sweet-smelling flowers visited by African sunbirds, which is equivalent to the hummingbird. The Mullers were sweet, gracious people; someone you would want to be your neighbor.

After breakfast, Mr. Muller got one of his workers to show them where the crude oil had been found. It was about ten miles south of his coffee plantation. They took one of the trucks and six of the German soldiers with them. When they reached the location, they found a large cenote, a large limestone sinkhole formation at the bottom of the sinkhole. There was a small deposit of crude oil and tar. After several days of exploring the surrounding rock formation and taking rock and oil samples, Wallace's father-in-law, Dr. Dunn, said, "I think it is a fluke. I cannot find any other signs that oil may be anywhere here in this area. I cannot explain why this crude has been collected in this limestone quarry. I'm going to recommend Leuna Oil Company to give up on this project. I believe the only oil here is the small deposit."

They drove back to Muller's farm. Mr. Muller took McKenzie, Dr. Dunn, and Wallace out on a driving safari. They were not that far from the Serengeti and Massai Mara. As they drove out on the plains of the Serengeti, McKenzie and Wallace were speechless. Wallace looked over at her, and tears were running down her cheeks. Both of them loved nature, and they were right in the middle of God's greatest migration. As far as you could see, thousands of animals were slowly moving north toward the Mara River. She looked at Wallace and said, "We are so blessed to see this. Very few people ever get to witness God's creation in motion."

Wallace said, "I'm blessed to have you and to be with you right now."

They camped overnight in the Serengeti. That night, Mr. Muller built a fire, and they sat and talked into the night. He told them many stories that happened to him and that had been passed down to him by native people who lived there.

The next morning, they drove back to the coffee plantation. Mr. Muller took them on a tour of the farm and told them that for the last two years, they have struggled because they have not got enough rainfall. Wallace asked him about irrigation. He responded, "If I were younger or if my son had not died, I would put in irrigation." He commented that he and his wife had been talking about selling the farm and moving back to Germany to be close to their daughter.

After lunch, Wallace asked McKenzie to go with him on a walk-through to the coffee grove. Wallace said, "McKenzie, I have been thinking, I can tell you love Africa, and I do too. I can't really explain it, but Africa draws you close to her like a mother or your wife."

McKenzie said, "I understand what you are saying. Africa is wild, free, and intoxicating."

Wallace asked McKenzie, "Would you like to live here someday?"

She said, "You may be surprised about what I am going to say! I could live here and never leave. I truly mean that with all my heart."

He said, "I believe you because I feel the same way. If it's okay with you, I'm going to ask Mr. Muller to give us the first chance if he ever decides to sell this farm." Later that day, McKenzie and Wallace sat down with the Mullers and told them that if they ever decide to sell the farm, they would like a chance to bid on it. They all shook hands and agreed.

The next morning, they loaded the trucks, exchanged embraces with their newfound Africa family (the Muller's), and headed back to Dar es Salaam. For their trip back to Europe, McKenzie and Wallace agreed they had found a new love and a new home—Africa.

When they returned to Europe, they made a stop in Hamburg, Germany, and met with Mr. Klaus of the Leuna Oil Company. Dr.

Dunn showed Klaus all the geological data that they had collected at the Endulen site. Dr. Dunn told Klaus that the small oil deposit at Endulen was a fluke of nature, and there was not enough oil in this deposit to send drilling equipment halfway across Africa. Klaus was extremely disappointed. He commented that Germany had a great need for petroleum, and we had not been able to locate any large deposits like the British and Americans.

"Klaus, we are sending another expedition to Namibia next spring, and I would like for you to head the expedition if you are interested."

Wallace said, "Yes, please keep us informed. McKenzie and I love Africa, and it would be an honor to lead another expedition for you, sir."

Wallace and McKenzie had been back in Scotland for six months when they received a letter from the Mullers in Africa. Mr. Muller had contracted malaria, and they were moving back to Germany. Mr. Muller had drawn up a contract and had a lawyer assign the deed of the land over to Wallace and McKenzie. In the contract, the Mullers owned 320 acres; they priced it to Wallace for five marks per acre. Wallace was to pay the Mullers 200 marks up front and one hundred marks per year until the balance was reached. Wallace and McKenzie had saved up enough money to make the down payment. They knew that the Mullers were basically giving them the farm for only a portion of what the cost should be. Wallace contacted one of his friends who was a lawyer and asked for his help in making sure everything was legally done and no one was taken advantage of.

In less than eight weeks, the money and deed to the farm in Africa had been delivered and settled.

At this time, Wallace and McKenzie both were working on a project for the Shell oil company. Mr. Dunn said he was bored, so he would travel to Africa and handle the transfer of the farm and stay there until Wallace and McKenzie could join him.

Wallace told McKenzie, "This is the second happiest day of my life, the first being the day that we were married."

McKenzie responded, "Yes, we have really been blessed by God. I know we will both love Africa."

Two months later, World War I began when Archduke Franz Ferdinand of Austria was assassinated, which caused Austria to declare war on Serbia. Germany sided with Austria, and Russia sided with Serbia. Within one week, France and Great Britain lined up to fight with Russia against Germany. The whole world had changed. The world was at war; Wallace and McKenzie's life would be drawn right into it.

Dr. Dunn had arrived at the coffee plantation in Endulen and took control of the farm. McKenzie had planned for Wallace and her to have a romantic dinner at a nice restaurant in Edinburgh. McKenzie had told Wallace she had a big surprise for him. When Wallace arrived at the restaurant, McKenzie was waiting on him. She had a radiant glow on her face, and she looked so beautiful. Wallace's eyes glistened like a child on Christmas morning. He said, "You promised me a gift, where is it?"

McKenzie said, "You are going to be a dad. I have expected it for weeks, but when I went to see Dr. O'Brien yesterday, he confirmed my suspicion." Wallace jumped up and grabbed McKenzie, picked her up, and swung her around.

He said, "You have made me the happiest man in the world."

Wallace said, "As soon as the child is born, I want us to move to Endulen."

McKenzie said, "That sounds good, but let's wait till the child is a couple of years old. I want to stay close to where I can call on Dr. O'Brien if we need him. Dad is loving being in Endulen and says he has the coffee plantation up and running and for us not to worry. He has everything under control. I'm ready to get back to Africa, but we are going to be parents, and we must put our child first."

Wallace said, "I agree, you always reason with your mind, where I often reason with my heart."

Chapter 4

War Breaks Out

Several weeks later, Wallace got some disturbing news from the British Defense Department. He was to report to a navy base at Caledonia. He was being called to serve in the British Navy.

It seemed like the whole world had gone crazy; all of Europe and Russia were at war. Wallace and McKenzie's lives and plans had been turned upside down and would be changed forever. McKenzie's dad was in Africa, and Wallace's parents lived in Auchleven. Wallace contacted his Aunt Ruth who lived in Edinburgh and asked her to check in on McKenzie occasionally.

Wallace reported to the navy base at Caledonia and started basic training. After several weeks of training, Wallace was moved to the Naval Intelligence Department at the base and began training in naval intelligence. He was promoted to a 1st lieutenant because of his test score and his college degree.

Wallace had been lucky to have been drafted by the Navy. If he had been drafted by the Army, he would probably have been assigned to the front lines in France or Belgium and be fighting in the trenches.

Two months later, Wallace received a letter while he was on board the British destroyer from McKenzie, telling him that he was a father. McKenzie had given birth to a healthy son, Rowan Wallace Leslie. Wallace and McKenzie had chosen the name Rowan as the child's first name before he had deployed to sea. Rowan had been McKenzie's grandfather's name.

The next two years, Wallace's ship, the Lance, sailed the ocean between England and France, protecting cargo ships convoys. The Lance was in the battles of Tekla, Dogger, and Jutland, and during the battle of Jutland, the Lance received minor damage from a shell from a German destroyer, and Wallace was injured when shrapnel from the blast severed part of Wallace's toes on his left foot. He was transported back to the naval base at Devonport in England. After several days in the hospital, he was surprised to see two visitors, McKenzie and Rowan. McKenzie said she had rented a room at a boarding house across the street from the hospital and would be staying in Devonport with Wallace until he recovered.

After Wallace recovered, he did not have to go back to sea but was transferred to an intelligent and security group complex in London where he was stationed for the rest of the war.

In December of 1918, Wallace, McKenzie, and Rowan boarded a ship in Brighton, England, and started their journey to their new home in Endulen, Africa.

Chapter 5

Home to Africa

Life was finally back to normal. McKenzie was more beautiful than ever, and Rowan was a beautiful healthy young boy. He favored his mom very much with black hair, blue eyes, and beautiful olive-colored skin.

The voyage was great with good food and service aboard the British ship, taking them two weeks to make it there. Once they arrived at Dar es Salaam, they purchased two BGC 29 British Crossley trucks to make their trip to Endulen. These trucks would be their lifeline to Arusha to move their coffee and other products to market in the future. McKenzie's dad had sent Karumba, the farm foreman, and three of his workers to help move the trucks and supplies from Dar es Salaam back to Eudenlen.

Everything had changed in Dar es Salaam since the war; there were no Germans here, but there were British troops everywhere. Many British citizens were moving from Europe to take the land that the British had seized from the Germans.

Wallace was thankful that McKenzie and he had purchased the land from the Mullers before the war. He was sure if the land had been owned by the Mullers instead of them, the British would have seized it from them.

They began their journey to their new home. They brought many of the items that they would need in their new home from England because you could not buy them in Africa. They loaded both of their trucks and started toward Eudenlen. Karumba told them it would probably take eight days to reach Endulen if they had no trouble. Karumba was a tall, strong man. His workers respected him and jumped when he gave a command. He seemed to be a good man and a good leader. As they drove across the savanna, Wallace reached over and took McKenzie's hand, and he said, "We are finally home."

She said, "Yes, thank God. He took care of you during the war, and He has always answered my prayers. It will be fine with me if we never have to leave Africa again."

Rowan was fascinated with the wildlife; he was like a child in a toy factory. When they would stop and take a break, Wallace would put a long cord onto a little harness he had made for Rowan so he could keep him close. There were so many dangerous creatures that could take his life in just a second. It would take Rowan, McKenzie, and Wallace some time to really feel comfortable in their new environment. Karumba warned McKenzie and Wallace to never let him play next to the large termite mounds that covered the landscape. Karumba warned them that all kinds of dangerous serpents lived in the large termite mounds. Many African children had lost their lives by sticking their hands into holes in the mounds. They had stopped under some trees to have lunch, and Karumba pointed out a tree. He said that the tree was called a euphorbia tree. They are African mill-sap trees; one drop of sap in your eye can make you blind for life. The only antidote is to get fresh breast milk from a woman who has recently given birth and put the milk into the eye. They all stayed clear of that tree. That night, they made their camp under some acacia trees on the open savanna. As they all set around the campfire, Karumba started to tell stories to Rowan about the animals of Africa.

He said, "God made the earth, He made large pools of water for the fish, the crocodiles, and the hippopotamus, and they all lived in these pools of water. One day, God was visiting one of these pools and noticed that most of the fishes were gone from the pool of water. He asked the crocodile, 'Did you eat the fish?' The crocodile said, 'No! I did not, but you may want to ask Mr. Hippopotamus.' God asked Mr. Hippopotamus, 'Did you eat the fish?' The hippopotamus was hesitant but said no. God said, 'One of you is lying to me.' He said, 'If I catch either one of you eating my fish, I will glue your mouth shut where you can never eat again.'"

Karumba then said, "Today, when we drove by the large pools of water, did you see the hippopotamuses open their mouths wide open toward the sky?"

Rowan said yes. Karumba said, "The hippopotamuses are show-ing God that they have no fish in their mouth". Karumba added, "One time, in a village near here, a little boy became extremely sick. The father of the little boy went to the local witch doctor and asked for help. The witch doctor told him he would help the boy if the father would pay him with a gold coin. The father had one gold coin, so he gave it to him. The witch doctor went into the forest and picked some herbs and mixed them. They gave the little boy the herbs, and he recovered. Several days later, the boy's sister became sick. The father went back to the witch doctor and said, 'My daugh-ter is sick, would you help me?' The witch doctor said, 'I will for another gold coin.' He replied, 'I gave you the only gold coin I had.' The witch doctor said, 'I'm sorry, but your daughter will die unless you can find another gold coin.'

"The father went into the forest and looked for herbs but could not find them. He set down on a rock and began to cry. A giraffe saw him crying and asked him what was wrong. The father told the giraffe his story, and the giraffe said, 'Don't cry. I will show you where the witch doctor picked the herbs. I have seen him go there many times before.' So the giraffe showed the father where the herbs were, and the father picked them. He gave them to his daughter, and she was cured. The witch doctor asked the father, 'Where did you get the herbs?' And the father said, 'The giraffe showed me where you would go to pick the herbs.' The witch doctor became terribly angry and went and found the giraffe and put a curse on him where he could never speak again. That is the reason that giraffes cannot make any noises, except he can only make a humming sound."

They passed through the herds of wildebeest and zebras and saw large numbers of elephants walking in single file heading toward the river. Rowan was totally captivated by the large variety and magni-tude of different animals that grazed and moved north. They realized he was witnessing his first northward migration of animals toward the Massai Mara. By looking into Rowan's eyes, they could tell he would love Africa. McKenzie and Wallace had made the right deci-sion many years ago when they decided to buy the farm at Endulen.

They finally arrived at home and were greeted by Dr. Dunn and the rest of the staff. Robert was glad to have his daughter back and was incredibly happy to see his grandson Rowan for the first time. The staff had prepared a feast for them, and Dr. Dunn had some local Maasai to come and perform a dance for the celebration of their return home. As they sat by the fire watching the Maasai jump high into the air and chant songs of their great battles and victories, McKenzie put her arm around Wallace and pulled him close. She said, "We are finally home. I don't ever want to leave. I want us to spend the rest of our lives here." She asked Wallace, "What are we going to call our new home?"

Wallace told McKenzie, "I have been thinking of a name and had asked Karumba, how do you say, God's Eden in Swahili? He told me Mungu Eden means God's Eden in Swahili. I had also asked him what the word Endulen means in Swahili, and he told me it means never give up."

McKenzie said, "Why don't we call our new home Mungu Eden?"

Wallace said, "I was hoping that was the name you would choose." Wallace took McKenzie's hand and said, "I give you all my love and ask God to always bless our new home, Mungu Eden."

Wallace stood up and asked for everyone's attention. He asked Karumba to translate for him. He said, "McKenzie and I have decided to call our new home Mungu Eden or God's Eden. This is our new home and everyone who works and helps us on the farm. This is your new home, and we are all God's children." Everyone at the feast cheered!

The next morning, Dr. Dunn showed McKenzie, Wallace, and Rowan around the farm. The coffee beans looked healthy, and the bushes were loaded with plump green coffee beans. Karumba told Wallace, "We will start the harvest in about four weeks." Dr. Dunn showed Wallace the irrigation system that he and Karumba had been working on. He said, "We hope to have it functional by next week."

Dr. Dunn told Wallace that a big male leopard had been killing the goats in the village and had killed one small calf. He said the village people were afraid it would take one of their children. "You and McKenzie always keep a close eye on Rowan. The big leopards are notorious for killing children here in East Africa." That night, Wallace and McKenzie had a long serious talk with Rowan about the dangerous lions, leopards, snakes, and hyenas that roamed the grasslands around the farm. Wallace instructed Rowan to never play outside alone unless he had adults close by. Rowan said he understood and that he had seen lions eating Buffalos and Gazelles on their trip to the farm.

The next day, Dr. Dunn suggested to Wallace and McKenzie that they let Khufu, Karumba's son, teach Rowan about the farm and the animals around the farm; the ones that are dangerous and the ones that are not. Khufu was twelve years old but already an experienced hunter and would often go with his dad on hunts that might last over a week. Wallace and McKenzie agreed that it would be best for Rowan to learn about his new environment from someone who had always lived here. The next morning, Karumba brought his son to meet Rowan. The two boys bonded quickly, and before long, Rowan was hunting wild guineas and fowls with Khufu. Khufu would take Rowan everywhere with him; he taught him about all the animals that lived near the farm. He taught him which snakes were poisonous and which ones were not. All of the training came naturally for Rowan; it was like he had lived in Africa his whole life. Somedays, Khufu and Rowan would leave early in the morning and not return until late evenings.

About six months after the Leslies had arrived in Africa, they all gathered one evening for dinner. McKenzie and the house staff had prepared a large meal. She asked her dad and Rowan to take a bath before dinner and dress in their best clothes. When everyone was seated, she said, "I have an important announcement to make. Rowan, you are going to be getting a baby brother or sister in about three months." Everyone was excited, and the staff sang a song of celebration. Rowan asked, "Will the birth be like what I and Grandfather witnessed at the barn the other night when the milk cow had a baby?" McKenzie hesitated, and she said, "Yes, but I'm no cow." Everyone laughed and celebrated into the evening.

The next morning at breakfast, Dr. Dunn told Wallace and McKenzie that they needed to come up with a plan for medical assistance when the baby was born if needed. Dr. Dunn said, "There is a Methodist missionary and his wife who have started a mission close to Ngorongoro Crater. I have heard that the wife of the missionary is a nurse, and she has helped many of the local people there, but that's twenty-six miles away from here. There is a doctor in Arusha, Dr. Andy Finley, who has a plane and will make house calls during emergencies."

Wallace said, "I believe in always being prepared. I will drive to Arusha and take McKenzie for a checkup and see what we would need to do to prepare a landing strip for the doctor's plane here on the farm. We really need one just in case we ever have an emergency, and I'm sure we might someday."

The next morning, Wallace, McKenzie, and Rowan loaded the truck for the trip to Arusha. Wallace asked Karumba to go with them just in case they ran into trouble and help show him the way to Arusha. Rowan asked if Khufu could go, and Wallace said sure.

When they arrived at the mission, the missionaries asked them to stay for the night. They said it was so seldom that they get any visitors and that it would be a treat. The missionaries were Daniel and Rita Sharp from America. Daniel had been a minister in Nashville, Tennessee, and his wife Rita had been a nurse. They had a calling to be missionaries when a missionary had spoken at their church. They had been at Ngorongoro for eleven months and already had an impact on the people who lived there. McKenzie told Mrs. Sharp that they were traveling to Arusha to see Dr. Finley for a checkup. Mrs. Sharp told McKenzie that she had helped deliver many babies before, and she would be glad to help if Wallace would come to the mission and get her when the time is near. McKenzie thanked her and said that she would like that very much and would send Wallace for her when the time was near.

After a good night's rest, the Leslies had a good breakfast with the Sharps and headed out east toward Arusha. They drove all day and reached Arusha at sundown. Dr. Dunn had told Wallace that he had a coffee grower friend in Arusha and had made arrangements for them to stay at his home while they visited the doctor. When they arrived, they were greeted by the Callahans who were the owners of the coffee plantation there in Arusha. They had moved to Arusha just before the war had ended, and they had bought the farm that some Germans had put up for sale.

The next morning, Wallace and McKenzie made a visit to Dr. Finley's while Rowan and Khufu stayed on the Callahan Farm and played with the Callahans' two sons.

Dr. Finley examined McKenzie and said everything looked okay, and there should not be any problems with the birth. Wallace asked Dr. Finley about how he could communicate with him if there was a problem and what he needed to do to prepare a landing field and runway to his specifications. "I will fly out to see you and McKenzie in about eight weeks and help you set up the radio, and I will let you borrow it until the baby is born. Then, I will pick it up and bring it back or sell it to you."

They thanked Dr. Finley and told him they would see him in eight weeks. Wallace guaranteed Dr. Finley that he would have the best landing strip prepared for him in Africa when he made his planned visit.

The next morning, Wallace and McKenzie thanked the Callahans for their hospitality and invited them to visit them soon at Endulen.

When the Leslies returned home, they were met by sadness; a child had been taken from the front porch of one of the huts of the Hadzabe tribe who lived on the farm. The child had been taken by a large male leopard; the same leopard the father of the child said who had taken some goats and the calf. Dr. Dunn told Wallace, "we need to go now and kill the leopard before it kills again." Wallace had not killed any large animals since he had lived at Eden and felt bad about having to kill the big cat, but he knew it had to be done. The next victim could easily be Rowan or McKenzie.

Dr. Dunn had sent word for Elias, a Maasai tracker and hunter, who used to work for Hans and Otto Meyers to come help them track and kill the large man-killer leopard. Dr. Dunn told Wallace to get his gun and gave Karumba a gun, for he was an experienced hunter and had hunted big cats before for Mr. Meyers. When Elias arrived, Wallace was struck by his size. He was close to six-foot-ten inches tall. His face had a scar, which looked like a claw mark. He was solid muscle; he had the look of a wild beast in his eyes. Wallace had never met anyone with a stature of a warrior like this before. All of the other Africans shied away from him or bowed in respect.

Dr. Dunn introduced Elias to Wallace. He stuck out his hand to shake, but Elias did not respond. Dr. Dunn said, "Wallace, you are looking at a real Maasai warrior who is strictly business." Dr. Dunn handed Elias a bag of coins and said, "Find the big cat." Elias only had a spear and a shield. He had red and yellow paint stripes on his face, chest, arms, and legs. He wore a headdress made from ostrich feathers.

Dr. Dunn told Karumba to show Elias the hut where the leopard had taken the child from. Wallace, Dr. Dunn, and Karumba followed Elias down the trail toward the hut. Rowan and Khufu started to follow, and Wallace yelled, "Get back to the house right now." They turned and started back toward the house.

Elias followed the big cat's trails to a small creek where they found the boy's bloody shirt. Elias then followed the trail up through some large boulders. He told Karumba that the cat was in the rocks above. He told Karumba to tell Wallace to stay where he was and cover the trail that he was on. He told Dr. Dunn and Karumba to go around to the other side of the big rocks and cover the other trail. He would go up into the rocks and drive the big cat out. Elias said in a joking manner to Karumba, "Tell your White friends to be careful and not to shoot me."

Chapter 6

The Child Killer

Elias started up the rock cliff beating his spear against his shield. Wallace thought to himself, *I have never seen anyone that brave to go up against a large leopard with a spear and shield.* Elias yelled, "I see him, he is heading toward you, Karumba." Just at that moment, Karumba saw the big cat heading toward him, then he saw Rowan and Khufu. They had followed the hunters and were between Karumba and the big cat. Karumba could not take the shot because he might hit one of the boys, so he ran toward the cat yelling. The cat jumped over the boys, landing on Karumba, biting into his neck and skull. Rowan and Khufu watched as the big cat ravaged Karumba. At that moment, Elias leaped from the rock above driving his spear through the big cat's chest. Dr. Dunn and Wallace arrived as Elias stabbed the cat several more times. Karumba and the big cat were both dead. The big cat had ripped Karumba's throat out and crushed his skull. Everyone was in shock. Karumba had given his life to save Khufu and Rowan.

Wallace yelled at Rowan and Khufu, "Your stupidity just got a good man killed, he gave his life to save yours." Wallace said, "Rowan and Khufu, go back to the farm and get some of the men to come to carry Karumba back to the farm." Elias said Karumba was a brave man and that he was his friend. Elias pulled out his knife and started to skin the leopard. He said, "I will tan and save the hide in honor of Karumba."

The next day, all the workers on the farm and people from the village nearby came by to show their respect for Karumba. He was well-known and a respected leader in the Hadzabe tribe. After Karumba's funeral, Wallace asked Elias if he would stay on at the farm and help. He told him that he and Dr. Dunn had been talking about running some hunting safaris out of the farm for rich Europeans to help pay for some of the farm expenses. Elias said that he would want to move his wives and children to the farm. Wallace asked, "How many wives do you have?"

Elias said, "I have six wives and eight children." Wallace told Elias that they would like to have them as neighbors. Wallace and Elias shook hands, and a new friendship began.

The following Monday, Wallace laid out the area he was going to put the landing strip on. He took all the workers from the coffee field and had them start picking up all the rocks and start leveling the landing strip. They cut all the trees on each end of the landing strip within two weeks. Wallace had a two-hundred-meter field that was smooth and level.

Wallace had to find someone to be the foreman over the workers at the farm. It would be hard to replace Karumba because the Hadzabe people had liked and respected Karumba because he was a good and fair man who treated all the workers with respect.

Wallace asked Elias if he would be interested in managing the workers on their coffee farm. Elias said, "No, I'm no farmer, I'm a warrior, a hunter, and that is women's work."

Wallace asked, "Do you know anyone who I could hire?"

Elias said, "There is a man who used to work for the Meyer brothers that I worked for. Everyone loves him, he is a good man and a Christian. He was raised by missionaries. He speaks German, English, and Swahili. They call him Angel." Wallace asked Elias if he would contact Angel and ask him if he would be interested in working as the farm manager. Elias said, "I will go tomorrow and find him. He is probably near Ngorongoro Crater."

The next day, Dr. Finley landed at the new airport without any problem. He gave McKenzie a good checkup and helped Wallace get the two-way radio set up and working. He left in time to make it back to Arusha before sunset. He told Wallace that the flight by air took only about thirty minutes, and Wallace said that is amazing.

Chapter 7

An Angel Appears

A couple of days later, Elias returned with Angel. The first time Wallace saw Angel, he was totally amazed. Angel actually had a glow about him! Wallace had never seen anyone who had a radiant glow about them. He asked Angel, "Are you a real angel?"

Angel said, "I just might be!" Elias told Wallace that Angel had run an excellent farm and production house for the Meyers brothers, and all the workers loved him at the coffee farm. Wallace asked Angel if he would be interested in running the coffee operation for him and McKenzie. Angel said, "If you will let me run this coffee farm the way I want to and let me choose the workers I want, I will give them housing, food, and a small wage. I promise you, I will give you the best coffee and the best coffee farm in Africa."

Wallace looked at Angel and smiled and said, "Angel, I believe you really will." Wallace added, "Angel, you are the new foreman, and I will help you any way I possibly can."

Elias walked up and said, "Wallace, what do you think?"

Wallace said, "I think you have brought me a real angel." Wallace turned back to ask Angel a question, and he was gone. Wallace turned back to look at Elias, and Elias said, "You know, his name is Angel."

A couple of days later, Rowan came running to the coffee orchard and yelled, "Dad! Mom needs you right now." When Wallace reached the house, McKenzie said, "It is time you need to call Dr. Finley." Wallace rushed to the radio and called for Dr. Finley. Dr.

Finley's nurse answered and said he would be right with him. Dr. Finley said, "Wallace, is that you?"

Wallace said, "Yes, it is time."

Dr. Finley said, "I will be there within one hour." Dr. Finley arrived and delivered a healthy baby girl, Emma McKenzie Leslie.

In a couple of days, the coffee harvest began. Angel had rearranged the workforce at the farm. He had only the women picking the coffee berries that were perfectly ripe. He had the men haul the beans to the harvest shed, wash, pick out any bean with an imperfection, then dry and husk them. Angel himself supervised the roasting of the beans. When Angel had finished processing his first batch of coffee beans, he ground a bagful then goes up to the house and prepares a pot for Wallace, McKenzie, and Dr. Dunn. As they savor the freshly brewed coffee, Dr. Dunn said, "This is actually the best coffee I have ever tasted in my life," and Wallace and McKenzie agreed. Angel smiled and said, "This is a little blessing from God to my new family."

As Angel processed the coffee, it was loaded into large burlap bags loaded on the trucks and started its journey to Arusha and, from there, onto Europe and the world.

In the next several years, Eden's coffee became one of the most sought-after coffees in Africa.

Chapter 8

Safari Walkabout

Several days later, Wallace saw a biplane circling the farm. Rowan and Khufu ran down to the landing strip and started waving some white banners they had prepared when they were expecting Dr. Finley. The plane lined up with the runway and slowly descended, touching down like a feather floating to the ground. The boys ran to greet the new visitors. A young man climbed out of the plane and asked, "Is this the Eden coffee farm?"

Rowan said, "Yes, sir! My name is Rowan, and this is my friend Khufu."

The young pilot said, "My name is Lorran Hicks, is your dad Wallace Leslie at home?

Rowan said, "Yes, sir, he is."

Lorran said, "Could I please meet him?"

Rowan and Khufu showed Mr. Hicks to the trail that led to the main house. As they approached, they were surrounded by a gang of young African children; all of them having to touch the airplane pilot. They had just seen him land in the field; it was almost like he was magic, and they wanted it to rub off on them.

When they reached the house, Wallace and McKenzie were sitting on the porch swing. Lorran introduced himself and explained that one of his friends, who was a safari guide, had told him about the Leslies' coffee plantation near Endulen. McKenzie got up and said, "I will fix you two, gentlemen, some of the world-famous Eden coffee. Lorran said, "Mr. Leslie, I will get right to the point why I am here. I would like to set up a safari base of operations here on your farm near your landing strip. You see, I'm a former British pilot without a current job. I and one of my friends are looking at opening up a hunting and sightseeing safari service in this area close to the Serengeti."

Lorran said, "It would be a great opportunity for both of us to make some really good money."

Wallace said, "Before I begin any new enterprise on this farm, I would have a talk with my wife, father-in-law, son, and the Hadzabe people who live on this farm with us."

Lorran said, "You mean that the Africans that live on this farm are part owners?"

Wallace said, "No! My wife and I own this farm, but the people who live here lived here long before we came, and they have the right to give us their opinion on any changes that we do to this land. It is where they live."

Lorran said, "Well, then can I meet with your family and the Hadzabe people?"

Wallace said, "Yes. First, McKenzie wants you to try some of our world-famous coffee."

Lorran took a sip and said, "Man, this is some more good coffee."

That evening, everyone was invited to the coffee barn, and food was served. Lorran got up and introduced himself. He presented his plan of setting a safari base of operations near the airfield. He said he will pay the Leslies well for the use of the land and offered to pay half of the expenses for a lodge that would have sleeping quarters for the guests and a warehouse to store all tents and camping supplies needed for a safari. He said he would give half the profits for the lodging and the food that the safari customers would spend to the Leslie family and Hadzabe people—divided equally. He told the Hadzabe people that he would need porters and camp personnel to prepare the food and transport the supplies to the camps out in the field, and he would pay them well. Wallace said, "We would like to privately discuss this! Can we let you know our answer tomorrow?" Lorran said that he would be glad to meet with them tomorrow. Wallace told Rowan to show Mr. Hicks to their guest house and make sure to take some cookies and coffee from the kitchen to the guest house.

That night, the Leslies and the Hadzabe people talked for hours. Wallace told them it would be a good opportunity for them to make some extra cash. He told them, "When the White hunters come, not all of them will be like me and McKenzie. Some may be cruel and rude and not treat the Hadzabe with respect." Some of them may even bring diseases." After a long discussion, Wallace held a vote. Almost all of the Hadzabe voted to build the safari camp next to the airstrip.

Wallace reminded Angel and the rest of the Hadzabe that the coffee production still came first and that working for the safari company could not interfere with their work on the coffee farm. They all agreed and pledged that the coffee came first.

The next morning, Wallace had Mr. Hicks come up to the main house for breakfast and said that he, his family, and the Hadzabe people had decided to try out this new safari adventure. Mr. Hicks went over the structured plan of the building layout with Wallace. Both men agreed and shook hands on the new venture.

Mr. Hicks asked Wallace if he had any well-experienced hunting guides. Wallace said, "We have the best guide and tracker in East Africa, Elias, he's a Maasai warrior, and he worked for the Meyers brothers. He was one of the first men who ever led safaris in this part of Africa."

Lorran asked Wallace, "Do you think that I could get Elias to take me on a walkabout down into Serengeti, and would you and Rowan like to go with me?"

Wallace said, "I'm sure Elias would take you! I can tell he really misses that part of his past life. I cannot go, but my son might be up to it if McKenzie does not object."

That night, Wallace told McKenzie that Lorran was taking Elias for a trek down into the Serengeti to look for possible hunting campsites, and he asked if her father and Rowan would like to go. McKenzie said no, but then she said, "Do you think Rowan is mature enough to go?"

Wallace said, "Rowan has matured so much in the last couple of years, and he is sixteen years old, yes, he is a young man, and he is a skilled tracker and hunter. Rowan is more African than European, and you know Africa is his home, and he knows it like the back of his hand." Two days later, Lorran Hicks, Dr. Dunn, Rowan, Khufu,

Elias, and two of Elias's sons began their trek to the Serengeti. Elias had two sons who were close to the same age as Rowan and Khufu. Elias led the party across the open savanna toward the Olduvai Gorge where a German, Dr. Wilhelm Kattwinkel, had found bones of prehistoric animals.

Rowan asked Lorran, "Do you think we will find any dinosaur bones at the Olduvai Gorge?"

Lorran responded, "We will just be passing through. We will not have time to really search."

Dr. Dunn responded to Rowan, "We might find something, Rowan, I have read several scientific studies about the site, and reports are it is rich in prehistoric fossils."

Rowan said, "I bet I will find a tyrannosaurus rex."

Khufu said, "What kind of animal is that?"

Rowan responded, "It's a large crocodile that weighed thirteen thousand kilograms." Khufu said a curse word.

Elias scolded him, "No cursing."

Khufu said, "That is one large lizard. I hope none of them are still around."

Dr. Dunn said, "Let's hope not, they all died off many years ago."

Khufu said, "If I see one, I'm going to pull a cheetah. All that you will see of me leaving will be a cloud of dust." Everyone laughed at Khufu's humor.

The group reached the Olduvai Gorge before sunset, set up camp, and started a fire. Elias told his two sons to get their bows and kill a couple of steenbok antelopes. They had seen some near a stream they passed earlier. Elias said, "Since we brought little food with us, we must eat off the land on this trip." Within less than thirty minutes, Jian and Kasi returned to camp with two steenbok antelopes. They quickly prepared the meat and put it on the fire to roast. Elias had Khufu and Rowan gather a good amount of firewood. He told Lorran and Dr. Dunn, "We have to keep the fire going all night, and someone will have to stay alert and on guard. The lions and hyenas will smell the fresh steenbok kill and may visit our camp tonight. If they get too close, just fire your weapon into the air, and they shall run away." Elias was right, at about two o'clock that night, some lions and hyenas started approaching the camp. Lorran fired his gun several times, and the lions left, but the hyenas kept coming back. Elias told Lorran to shoot one of the hyenas; he did, and the bullet killed it. The other hyenas tore the dead hyenas apart and ate him. Khufu said, "Those are some ugly, nasty demons to eat one of their own like that."

Elias said, "They are more vicious than a lion, and they often kill lions." He told them that, oftentimes, when a human died and was buried in the grave, the hyenas would dig the body up and eat it. Khufu said, "I could tell that those hyenas had been eating something rotten because they smell rancid. Probably one of those old tyrannosaurus rexes you were talking about."

The next morning, Elias got everyone up at daybreak. He said, "We have a full day ahead of us, and I have a surprise for all of you. We will be trekking right by the Ol Doinyo Lengai, the mountains of god. Dr. Dunn, you may have heard of it, they call it the black sand dune of Africa.

Dr. Dunn said, "Yes, Elias, I have heard about it and read about it, some of the native people call it barran. It's a large black magnetic sand dune that moves across the African savanna, its size is about sixty meters by thirty meters and three and a half meters high. The Maasai and other local natives used to worship it as a god and would sacrifice their children on it."

Elias said, "That is true, you have to see it to believe it." When they reached the black sand dune, there it was like Dr. Dunn had described. The black sand is magnetic, so as the wind blew it across the savanna, it sticks together like small magnetic balls. Dr. Dunn said, "The large black sand dune moves about two to three meters a year."

Elias said, "You, boys, can climb on it if you want, it will not swallow you up like some of the old legends tell." Rowan slowly climbed up on the dune, and Dr. Dunn followed. Rowan called to Khufu, "Come on up!" Khufu was hesitant but slowly climbed to the top of the dune. He called out to Jian and Kasi to climb up on the dune, but they said, "No! That is child's play." Rowan noticed that Elias did not get close to the dune either. He understood there were many stories in the native folklore of witches, demons, and the unexplained. Once the boys were off the dune, Khufu said, "I knew that big black sand god was thinking about eating us, but we smell like hyenas. So Barran said, 'I will wait on some boys that smell better.'"

They all stood for a while in amazement at the marvel of nature and thought about all the children who had been sacrificed on the black sand dune.

They then gathered their supplies and moved toward the Serengeti. They reached the tall grass of the Serengeti that the Swahili people called "swand grass." Elias told all of them to fall into a single line. He asked Lorran to come to the front of the line with his .500 Nitro Express double-barreled rifle, and he asked Dr. Dunn to cover the rear of the line.

Chapter 9

Lion Attack

You may walk right up a pride of lions sleeping or eating in the tall grass without realizing it until it is too late. Elias had his spear but also was carrying a British Lee-Enfield .303 rifle, and Rowan was carrying a .404 Jeffery. As they walked across the savanna, Elias would jump straight up into the air to get a better visual perspective of the savanna around them. He told Lorran, "We need to get out of this tall grass because this grass was as tall as his chests." Elias held up his hand and clenched his fist, and he whispered, "Everyone, stand still." They had walked right into a pride of sleeping lions. There were about twelve to fourteen adult lions. They had killed a young African buffalo, feasted, and were sleeping. Elias motioned to everyone to back up slowly in a single file. He said, "If a lion charges, fire and reload." As they were backing up, watching, and waiting for a charge, Dr. Dunn tripped over some tall grass and fell down. The sound of him falling alerted the lions, and part of them ran into the grass. Elias said, "Everyone, be ready, we may have a charge of more than one lion." They alertly and cautiously backed through the trail in the tall grass that they had created. Before they had entered the tall grass, they had been walking down a dry streambed about two hundred meters away from where they had encountered the pride of lions. Elias told them to keep moving back toward the streambed; he said they would be much safer in the open. When they reached the streambed, the bank of the streambed was about twelve meters above the dry stream. Elias told Kasi to lead them up to an animal trail that cut a path to the dry streambed.

When they all made it down in the streambed, Elias said, "Everyone, go to the center of the stream and make a circle." He added, "I have seen at least two of the big female cats trying to flank us, be ready if they charge. Aim straight and shoot to kill." Everyone had their guns pointed toward the high bank where they had just descended from the tall grass. They saw a large female lion crouching at the edge of the grass getting ready to lunge toward them. Elias said, "Lorran, do you have her in your sight?" Lorran said yes. He said, "On the count of one, you and I will fire, the rest of you, save your bullets in case we have another charge." Elias and Lorran fired at the same time. The cat jumped straight up and fell back into the grass. Elias said, "Everyone, be ready, we may see another charge." At that point, they could see a large male and several females approaching the dead lioness. Elias said, "Everyone, just stay steady, don't fire unless I tell you." The large male approached the dead female, licked her face, rubbed his head against her head, and slowly walked back into the tall grass. The other female lions did the same; they walked up to her and licked or smelled her and walked away. Elias said, "I think we are going to be okay now." He said, "You never know about lions. By those lions having a full stomach of buffalos, they will probably just go back to the tall grass and sleep until they are hungry again."

Rowan thought back to when the leopard had killed Karumba when Karumba had saved his and Khufu lives. He felt sad for the pride of lions. The large female lion would still be alive if they had not cut across the high grass to save time. He could tell the lions felt loss and sadness when the large male lion had licked the lioness's face and stroked his head against her and the other young lionesses who had come by to show their respect. Were they the lioness's sisters or maybe her daughters?

Death was an everyday occurrence in Africa. All the animals had to eat; some were vegetarians, others were carnivores. It was the way God had set up this beautiful creation that Rowan loved so much. Rowan was always sad to see an animal or people suffer and die, but it was the world that he lived in, and even with all of the death, there was birth and new life; he loved Africa. He looked up toward the sky and thanked God for his blessings.

Elias told Dr. Dunn and Lorran, "That was a close call! I should not ever have taken you into the high grass."

He said, "We will follow the dry riverbed until we reach an area that has better visibility."

That evening, the travelers set up camp at a kopje, a large rock outcropping on the Serengeti. Elias said he felt bad about what had happened today, and he told Rowan, Lorran, and Dr. Dunn that he knew they had not slept well since they had left Eden. He cut grass and fixed them a bed between two large boulders. He had Kasi and Jian cut some thornbushes and built a Boma around the camp. He said, "I, Jian, and Kasi will take turns guarding the camp tonight, we will keep the fire going, and we should not be bothered by lions or hyenas tonight."

That night was uneventful. Rowan awakened to the smell of fresh springbok antelope roasting on the open fire and fresh coffee brewing. As he was putting on his shoes, he heard his grandfather yelling and cussing. Elias ran behind the large boulder to see what was wrong with Dr. Dunn. Elias came back carrying a six-foot dead black mamba snake. Dr. Dunn followed him still cursing and thanking God at the same time. Dr. Dunn said he had gone behind the rock to relieve his bowels. He squatted down to relieve himself, and something hit him in the leg. Luckily, the snake bite had not penetrated the thick leather of Dr. Dunn's knee-high boots. Elias warned the group to always check an area before sitting down. Elias said the black mamba was probably hunting for the rock hyrax, a small rodent that lives in the kopjes formations. He told them that if the black mamba's fangs had penetrated Dr. Dunn's boots, he would have been dead in less than twenty minutes. After that, they were all more careful where they stepped or sat.

Lorran told Elias and Dr. Dunn that he was satisfied with the trek that they had taken and had picked four ideal campsites for the upcoming safaris that he and Wallace would be organizing as soon as they could get the lodge and warehouse built.

Chapter 10

Elias's Night Out

Elias and his sons broke camp, and the group of trekkers headed east toward Endulen. That afternoon, they reached a small Maasai village. Elias and his sons were kin to some of the Maasais that lived there. The chief welcomed them to come into his home, an *inkajijik*. The inkajijik is a circular structure built out of sticks woven together to form a complete circular structure. The structure is then covered with mud and cow dung. The entrance of the structure winds around the structure with a passage only large enough for one person to pass through at a time; this prohibits a group of people from rushing into the building all at one time. It also makes it easier to defend against an animal such as a lion trying to enter.

The Maasai believe that God gave them all of the cattle of Africa, and this represents a sacred bond between God and the Maasai. As they entered the chief's home, they had to turn sideways to pass through the narrow passageway of the hall entrance. Once, however, when they were inside the structure, there was plenty of room. A small wooden cooking stove was in the center of the room, but there was no chimney or ventilation, so the room was very smokey, and the smells of cow dung and body odor were prevalent. The chief welcomed them, and he started a small fire. As the glow of the fire amplifies the room, to their surprise, six young women sat on a grass mat in the corner of the hut covering their faces with colorful veils. The chief said, "This is six of my young wives."

Dr. Dunn said, "How many wives, do you have?"

"Besides these wives, I have four older wives." The chief said with a smile, "I like the younger ones better, they do not talk back to me yet," and he let out a big laugh, and they all laughed with him.

One of the young wives' hands (each of them) a clay dish and took a gourd and dipped a type of soup out of a large pot next to the fire. Dr. Dunn asked Elias, "What is this?"

Elias responded, "It is like your cream of wheat, but it is made from milo." He said, "It is good, don't insult the chief by not eating it." As Rowan tasted the food, he wanted to spit, but he swallowed it anyway.

After they finished eating, the Maasai men and women did a ritual dance in the center of the village. They were quite good and entertaining. After they were entertained, the chief told them that they could sleep in his home that night, and he would sleep with his older wives. He asked them if they would like a woman to sleep with. Dr. Dunn and Lorran said, "Thank you, but we are married," which they were not. "Our faith does not allow us to have more than one woman."

The chief laughed and said, "You need to be a Maasai for one night. It's good to have many wives." He looked at Rowan and Khufu and said, "Do you want a woman?"

Dr. Dunn said, "No! They are already promised."

Khufu said, "Man, I would have said yes if your grandfather had been quiet." Elias stood and took the hands of two of the young women, and they followed him out into the darkness. The next morning, they thanked the Maasai for their hospitality and packed up to leave. Elias came out of one of the huts followed by the two women. He stretched his tall, slender body and yawned.

Lorran said, "Good morning, sleepyhead, how did you sleep?"

Elias's responded, "I or neither one of the young women slept any last night." As Elias started to walk toward them, the two women grabbed him and tried to pull him back inside. He told them he must go home to his wives but promised them he would be back to visit. Dr. Dunn asked Elias if the chief would be upset or jealous that he had slept with two of his wives last night. Elias said, "No, he probably needed a break anyway." Elias said it was an old custom among the Maasai warriors to travel and stop at a Maasai village; he may take any woman he wanted for the night. He said the warrior would take the woman's hand he wanted to be with, and she would take him to her hut. He would stick his spear in the ground outside the hut, and no one was allowed to bother them as long as the spear remained in the ground outside the hut.

Dr. Dunn said, "Well, if you had a pretty, attractive young wife, you would have to keep her behind closed doors all the time."

Elias said, "That is so true, Doctor, many of the Maasai that have a woman who is beautiful and doesn't want them to sleep with another man will ban their wives from coming out of their hut when a visiting man enters the village. If you remember yesterday, when we arrived at the village, you saw very few young women out in the village. Their husbands had restricted them to stay inside."

Lorran said to Elias, "How many children do you have scattered over Africa?"

Elias responded, "More than most men."

Kasi led the trekkers down the trail that led to Endulen. Elias brought up the rear. They reached a stream with large boulders; Elias warned everyone to be careful crossing the stream. He said, "There are some big crocodiles and hippos around here." He told Kasi, "Let me take the lead, the vegetation is thick, and the trail narrows to a small path, almost like a tunnel through the thick vegetation."

Elias said, "I don't like this. This is the hippos' trail, and if we run head-on into one, there will be no place to run." Elias told everyone to back up, and he would find a better trail for them to follow. When Elias reached the stream, he told everyone to follow him. After a few minutes, Elias located a large trail that was much safer. As the men moved through the thick vegetation, they came to a boulder-covered hill. Elias said, "We will go around this instead of trying to climb it." As Elias reached a sharp curve in the trail, he held his hand up and clenched his fist. A half-grown wildebeest lay in the trail, fresh blood was oozing out of the fresh claw and teeth marks on its neck. Elias said, "There is a leopard near, and it may attack at any time if he thinks we are trying to take his meal." He told everyone to back up slowly and be ready to fire. He said, "Leopards are so fast, you will never see them coming before they are up on you. We will all move slowly back to the stream and find another trail that bypasses the leopard and the hippo trail."

Chapter 11

Blackwater Fever

Dr. Dunn complained. He said, "I think I have picked up some kind of virus." He added, "I'm running a fever and aching all over."

Elias said, "I know where there is an old deserted homestead. We will stop there and rest for the night." Once the travelers reached the homestead, Kasi built a fire in the fireplace, and Jian went out to find some game for dinner. Rowan found some old blankets and took them to his grandfather.

Dr. Dunn said, "I'm freezing, it is a beautiful, warm summer day, and I'm freezing."

Elias bent over and looked into Dr. Dunn's eyes and said, "I'm sorry to tell you, Doctor, but you have malaria."

Dr. Dunn said, "I was afraid of that, I have not felt good in several weeks."

Elias said, "We need to get you home as soon as possible, and you need to see the White doctor who flies by plane."

Elias sent Kasi to find some saa-wawa plants. He told Dr. Dunn the Maasai had used this plant for generations to treat malaria.

Kasi soon returned with a small pouch full of leaves. Elias grounded the leaves between two stones and put them into a cup of hot water. When the water cooled, he gave it to Dr. Dunn and told him to drink it. Elias said, "This will make you feel better, stop the fever, and make you sleep."

The next morning, Dr. Dunn woke up and told Elias he felt much better. Elias prepared him another cup of the saa-wawa to drink, and they headed out toward Endulen. The travelers reached Eden shortly after sundown. Dr. Dunn was burning up with a fever again; this time he was much worse. McKenzie wrapped her dad in blankets and gave him some quinine tablets that she brought from Scotland. Elias told McKenzie that they must get Dr. Dunn to Arusha tomorrow to Dr. Finley, or he would get worse.

Lorran told Wallace and McKenzie that he would fly Dr. Dunn to Arusha first thing tomorrow morning. Rowan begged his mom to please let him go with his grandfather in case Dr. Finley wanted him to stay. Wallace and McKenzie agreed that it would be best. Dr. Dunn would need someone to watch out for him, and it would be a good experience for Rowan because he had only been off the plantation a few times in his lifetime.

The next morning, Dr. Dunn seemed to be getting worse. Wallace and Lorran helped him into the airplane. Lorran told Rowan that he would have to sit in the back seat with his grandfather. It was a tight fit, but Rowan was able to squeeze into the back seat.

As the plane took off from Eden, Wallace, McKenzie, and all the workers on the farm were there to wave goodbye to Dr. Dunn and Rowan as they flew toward the rising sun in the east. It took less than an hour to reach Arusha's airfield. Lorran called Dr. Finley's office, and Dr. Finley drove to the airport and picked them up. He took them back to his office and started treating Dr. Dunn. Dr. Finley asked Dr. Dunn, "Is this the first time you have had these symptoms?"

Dr. Dunn said, "No, I have been having some minor spells for about six months."

Dr. Finley said, "Robert, you should have mentioned it to me when I was out at your farm last time. Undoubtedly, you have had malaria for some time. Sometimes, someone with malaria has very mild symptoms for several months or even several years, then it will just get a whole lot worse overnight. Sometimes, stress will bring it on, a bad case like this, have you been stressed lately?"

Dr. Dunn said, "Well, Rowan, Lorran, and I have just walked halfway across East Africa on a walking safari. We just got back last night."

Dr. Finley said, "Well, that is what probably triggered it, plus, I'm sure you were not drinking clean water."

Dr. Dunn said, "No, we were getting our water out of streams, but we were boiling it."

Dr. Finley said to Robert, "I hate to be the one to tell you, but I think you have blackwater fever, and no telling what else. Rowan, do you and Lorran feel okay?"

They both replied, "We feel good."

Dr. Finley said, "Well, you are a lot younger, and your immune system is probably a lot better than your grandfather." Dr. Finley said, "This is not good, I will fly you to Dar es Salaam or Lorran can. The military has a hospital set up in Dar es Salaam. They can give much better treatment than I can here in my office. I hate to be the one to tell you this, Robert, but you may have waited too long to seek treatment. May God be with you. I will call the hospital in Dar es Salaam. I have several good friends who are doctors there. I will tell them to give you the best treatment possible. I will have an ambulance pick you up at the airport and transfer you to the hospital. Good luck, old friend, may God bless your stubborn soul."

In less than two hours, Lorran, Rowan, and Dr. Dunn landed at the Dar es Salaam airport. An ambulance was waiting on them and took them straight to the hospital. The doctors were waiting on them and took Dr. Dunn straight to a room. One of Dr. Finley's friends came into the room. He said, "My name is Dr. Ross, I will be treating you, Dr. Dunn. I just want to be honest with you, this will be an uphill battle, I think I can honestly say you have about a fifty percent chance of making it, but you look like a fit man for your age."

Rowan said, "My grandfather will beat it, he is one of the strongest men I have ever known."

Dr. Ross said, "A positive attitude goes a long way with this disease, I believe he will make it."

Dr. Ross told Rowan and Lorran that they both looked tired and needed to go home and get some rest. Dr. Ross said, "This is going to be a long-drawn-out process."

Rowan said, "Lorran, my granddad and I just got back from a ten-day walking trek to the Serengeti."

Dr. Ross said, "Dr. Dunn, is that true in your condition?"

Dr. Dunn said, "Yes, the virus did not affect me until we were almost home."

Dr. Ross said, "Robert, you are one tough cookie, if you just walked across East Africa with blackwater fever, I'm sure you can walk out of this hospital in a couple of weeks."

Lorran told Dr. Dunn, "I have a home near the beach. If it's okay with you, I'm going to take Rowan with me and try to get some good rest. We will come back and check on you tomorrow."

Rowan said, "I will stay here with Granddad."

Dr. Dunn said, "No, Rowan, go with Lorran, none of us have had any sleep in over a week. It will do us all good to have some time alone and rest."

Rowan said, "Okay, I will see you tomorrow."

Lorran said, "I will get in touch with Wallace and let him know we are here, and everyone is okay."

Dr. Dunn said, "Thank you."

Chapter 12

Ladan

Lorran called a cab, and he and Rowan got in, and he told the cab where to go, and they drove through town. Rowan was amazed that Dar es Salaam had grown and changed so much since the last time he was there. The cab arrived at a nice villa next to the ocean. Lorran said, "We are home." It was a beautiful beachfront home with palm trees growing on the beach. The water was a beautiful turquoise blue. Rowan said, "If I lived here, I would never leave."

Lorran said, "You told me the same thing about Eden."

Rowan said, "I would still like to live in Eden, but it would be nice to have a vacation beach house here too."

Lorran said, "Yes, the best of both worlds." As Lorran and Rowan entered the back door, Lorran yelled, "Honey, I'm home." Rowan was shocked, he thought Lorran lived alone.

A voice called back, "I'm on the sunporch."

Lorran told Rowan to put his bags over on the chair. "I want to introduce you to Ladan, she takes care of my home for me when I'm away and takes care of me when I'm home." As Rowan dropped his bags and turned, he saw one of the most beautiful women he had ever seen in his life. Lorran introduced her. He said, "This is Ladan, and, Ladan, this is my friend Rowan." She walked over and ran her fingers through Rowan's black hair and said, "Where did you find this young man?"

"Ladan, this is my new business partners' son, Rowan."

Ladan said, "Rowan, welcome to our home. Our home is your home, we will make sure your visit is memorable, if you need anything at all, just let us know." Lorran showed Rowan where the bath is and said, "You take a good bath and try to get some sleep. I will take you back to the hospital tomorrow."

Rowan said, "I don't mean to be rude, Ladan. You're so beautiful, what nationality are you?" Ladan said her father was French, and her mom was Somalian.

Lorran said, "Yes, she is incredibly beautiful, and she has a free spirit about her. Don't let her frighten you! She may be a little flirty with you and even try to embarrass you, but that's just her nature. She is attracted to younger men, sometimes, I worry she may leave me someday for a younger man. But if she does, I will never regret the time that she has shared with me. Sometimes, I may be gone for weeks, but she is always here when I get home. I don't know if she loves me or if she loves my home. I do know she is the most beautiful, intriguing, and passionate woman that I have ever known. I think she has already gone to bed, so I'm going to take a good bath and pull an Elias. Sleep well, my young friend."

After a long soaking bath, Rowan was lying in his bed thinking of his grandfather. His mind drifted to Ladan and Lorran. He wondered what they were doing; he let his imagination drift. He fantasized that he was lying next to the most beautiful woman he had ever seen; she was running her hands through his long black hair. Then, he heard someone knocking at the door. Rowan heard a policeman tell Lorran that someone had broken into his warehouse at the dock and had started a fire. The policeman said they had arrested the man, and they needed Lorran to come down and file charges against him and look at the damage done to the warehouse. Lorran told Ladan he would be back as soon as possible.

Rowan heard the door shut and a car driving away, then he heard someone walking in the house. He wondered if Lorran had come back, then his bedroom door opened slowly, and he could see Ladan. She had on a nightshirt but nothing more. She said, "I'm cold, can I lay next to you?" Rowan felt a cold sweat pop out on his skin. She started to play with his hair, running her fingers through it. She said, "Are you okay?" He put his hand on her leg and began to stroke it. She asked, "Are you scared?"

"Yes," he said kindly.

She said, "Don't be, I will be gentle." Ladan said, "How old are you, Rowan?"

He said, "I'm sixteen. I will be seventeen in August." Ladan pulled Rowan close and slowly kissed his lips; he caressed her breasts. He thought, *Am I dreaming, or is this real!* He pinched himself and wondered, *Is this really, really real?*

Ladan asked Rowan, "Have you ever made love to a woman?"

Rowan said no, but he said, "When I saw you today, I wanted to make love to you."

Ladan said, "I thought I saw that look in your eyes."

Ladan told Rowan to just lie still. She said, "I'm going to get on top of you. I will be really gentle." Ladan slowly straddled Rowan and started swaying back and forth.

Rowan said, "I love you."

She said, "Don't say that, this is not love!" Ladan passionately kissed Rowan. He started to put his hands around the curve of Ladan's back and pulled her close to him. They were one. Rowan had this wonderful feeling, flooding his body with endorphins. He had never felt anything like this before. Ladan lay down beside Rowan and said, "Put your arms around me, I need someone to hold me. Lorran had been gone for weeks. I just need you to hold me." Rowan drifted into a deep sleep. He heard the back door open; he felt for Ladan, but she was gone. He then heard Ladan and Lorran giggling, then he heard Ladan telling Lorran not to stop. Then, everything was quiet. Had this been a dream, Rowan smelled of the pillow; her fragrance was still present. He drifted off into a deep sleep. He had flown halfway across Africa and made love to the most beautiful woman he had ever met. He wondered what tomorrow would hold for him!

The next morning, Lorran woke Rowan up and said breakfast was ready. He said, "We will be eating on the sunporch deck." Rowan quickly bathed, combed his hair, and walked onto the sun deck. The fresh morning breeze of the ocean air was refreshing. Ladan and Lorran were sitting at the breakfast table eating fruits and having coffee. Lorran asked Rowan, "How did you sleep last night?"

Ladan said, "I bet he slept like a baby."

Rowan said, "I did sleep well. I had this wonderful dream about this beautiful African princess."

Lorran said, "We don't have time for fairy tales, eat your breakfast quickly. I'm going to show you where to catch a cab. I will ride with you to the hospital to see your grandfather, then I'm going to have to fly up to Nairobi to meet an investor to help finance the safari camp we are going to build on your family's farm. I will be back tomorrow afternoon, then if your grandfather is doing better, I need to fly back to Eden to see your dad, and you can ride with me. I'm going to give you some cash for taxi fare and food if you have to buy anything. Ladan will be here, so you can come back to the house anytime if you get bored at the hospital."

Rowan ate an apple, a banana, and a cup of coffee. Rowan told Ladan, "I will send some of my family's coffee back with Lorran, you will love it." Rowan and Lorran walked to the street corner and caught a cab to the hospital. Lorran told Rowan, "There is always a cab at the hospital, so you can get a ride anytime of the day." When they arrived at the hospital, Dr. Dunn seemed to be doing better. Lorran said, "I'm glad we got you here when we did."

Dr. Dunn said, "You probably saved my life by flying me here. I will always be grateful." Lorran told Dr. Dunn that he was flying to Nairobi and would not be back until tomorrow. He said, "Rowan knows where my house is, and he can stay there tonight."

Lorran said, "My friend Ladan lives there with me, and she will make sure Rowan has plenty of food to eat. She is really a good cook, maybe when you get to feel better, you can meet her. She's a wonderful woman." Rowan walked with Lorran to the door and thanked him for helping save his grandfather. Lorran said, "Your grandfather still has a long way to go before he can go back home." As Lorran started to walk away, he said, "Don't let Ladan intimidate you, sometimes she can be demanding. She is a special woman sometimes, she reminds me of one of the big cats more than a woman, and I like that about her. She has an inner wild side, but she can also be very loving, and she has a kind heart. I will see you the day after tomorrow."

Rowan replied, "Be safe."

Rowan walked back to Dr. Dunn's room, and they talked for a while. Dr. Dunn said, "We are fortunate that Lorran was at the farm when I got sick, or I might not have made it to the hospital." Rowan asked his grandfather if he could get him anything. Dr. Dunn said, "No, I'm okay." He asked, "Rowan, you seem nervous, is everything okay?"

Rowan replied, "Yes, everything is good." He said, "Granddad, Lorran lives in a beautiful beach house right on the beach. If you are feeling okay, can I go back and hang out at the beach? I have never been to an ocean but once before in my life."

Dr. Dunn said, "Sure, just be careful. You know the city has wild beasts like the jungle does, but they are two legged."

Rowan said, "I promise to be careful." Rowan ran to the taxi stop and told them the address he wanted to go to. When Rowan reached Lorran's house, he entered the back door and called out Ladan's name, but no one was at home. He felt depressed; he was hoping Ladan would be there waiting on him.

He walked out and walked toward the ocean. He saw Ladan sitting in a lawn chair on the beach. She was wearing a le pagne around her waist. It's like a short wraparound skirt. Ladan was not wearing a top; her breasts were exposed. She looked up at Rowan and said, "What are you staring at? Have you never seen a woman's breast? African women are different from European women. African women are proud of what they have been blessed with, and European women try to cover their most beautiful features. Do you think I am beautiful?"

Rowan said, "Yes, unbelievably beautiful." Ladan asked Rowan if he would like a drink. He said sure. She poured a fruit-like punch out of a thermos and handed Rowan a cup. He tasted the drink and said it's very good. She said it was pineapple and rum.

Ladan said, "Rowan, why are you here and not at the hospital?" She added, "I know why you are here, you enjoyed what happened last night, and I did too. But you have to know, I have no feelings for you. I am Lorran's woman. He takes good care of me, he gives this beautiful home to live in, he gives me money, and lets me live the life I want to live. I love Lorran, but he is never here, I have always been true to him, we have been together for four years. However, I am a woman, and I have needs, just like last night when Lorran left. I did not know when he would come back home, and you were convenient. Now, Lorran is gone again, and you are here, would you like to make love to me again?"

Rowan said, "Yes, I would."

She said, "Well, we will today, tonight, and tomorrow. But I want you to understand something, I am Lorran's woman, and if you ever try to come between us or show me affection or try to flirt or touch me in front of Lorran, I will hurt you badly."

Ladan got up from her chair and took Rowan's hand and said, "Follow me. I will teach you how to please a woman." When they reached the bedroom, Rowan started ripping his clothes off. Ladan said, "Stop, all of you, European men, are the same, always in a hurry. You can learn something from the African women. Pole, pole—pole, pole," which in Swahili means slowly. "Savor each moment, think about each kiss before you kiss your lover. Plan every motion of your hand before you touch your lover." Ladan slowly caressed Rowan's neck, then she slowly kissed his lips. She took his hand and very gently pulled his fingers across her breasts. She said slowly, "Slowly now, isn't that much more sensuous, Rowan?"

He said, "Yes, I like that much better."

Rowan spent very little time at the hospital while Lorran was gone. When Lorran arrived home, he asked Rowan, "How is your grandfather?"

Rowan said, "About the same."

"What have you been doing while I was gone?"

Rowan said, "Hanging out at the beach."

"Has Ladan been nice to you?"

Rowan said, "Yes, she has been a nice hostess. I really like it here in Dar es Salaam. On my next holiday, I would like to come back and visit with you and Ladan again."

Lorran said, "There probably will not be any holidays for a while. As soon as we get that safari service up and running, it will consume all of the spare time. We already have clients lined up and waiting for us to open."

Lorran and Rowan caught a cab to the hospital and visited Dr. Dunn. Afterward, they flew on to the farm at Eden. As they were flying, Lorran asked Rowan, "What do you think of Ladan?"

Rowan responded, "I think she is a very special, unique person. She is very independent and has a mind of her own, and she loves you, Lorran. She told me she did. She said she was your woman only. She said you are a good man and gave her everything that she could ever want, and she loved the beach home on the ocean."

Chapter 13

The Safari Company

When Lorran and Rowan reached Eden, Lorran told Rowan, "I would like for you to set in on the meeting with me and your dad. This new company is going to be a partnership between your dad and me, and I hope in the future you will also become a partner."

Rowan said, "Can I be a partner now?"

Lorran said, "How much money do you have that you can invest right now?" Rowan said not very much. Lorran said, "You will just have to work your way in slowly."

When Lorran and Rowan reached the house, Wallace and McKenzie were sitting on the front porch. McKenzie grabbed Rowan's arm and said, "You better give your mom a hug."

Rowan gave her a quick hug and said, "Lorran and I have some business to discuss with dad."

McKenzie said, "Excuse me, who made you chief of this tribe?" She then said, "Rowan, help me get a couple of chairs from the house and bring them out on the porch where you, men, can discuss business, and I will make some fresh tea."

Wallace asked, "Rowan how is your grandfather?"

Rowan said he seemed to be improving, and McKenzie said, "Thank God."

As Wallace, Lorran, and Rowan sat down in a chair around the little table on the porch, McKenzie brought them three glasses of tea.

Lorran said, "I have some good news. I just got a nice size loan from some British investors in Nairobi. It will be enough to build the lodge and warehouse and buy a passenger plane to bring in our new clients. I have hired a chef from one of the safari lodges in South Africa who has four years of experience. We will set up two permanent camps, and we will have one portable camp that we will use to follow the migration in the Serengeti.

"I plan on using Elias as a head guide, and I was impressed with his two sons, Kasi and Jian, and I want to work them into being guides also. I would like to ask you and McKenzie for your approval, but I would like to make Rowan a camp manager and guide, he is a natural, and someday soon, I would like to work him in as part owner.

"I would like to offer hunting safaris where we will guide a hunter for a set price with a designated list of animals he can hunt and the price of each animal he kills. Rowan has shown an interest in leading photo safaris, I think we can make just as much money on photo safaris as hunting safaris. There are going to be a lot of people from Europe and even Americans who will pay good money for the African adventure.

I purchased a 1930 Stinson trimotor plane, which will hold ten passengers, also, I bought three 1930 Mercedes Benz SSK touring cars."

Wallace said, "We are not going to have to mortgage the farm, are we?"

Lorran said, "No, it's all on an open note. The investors know, we have gotten a gold mine, and they want in on the action."

Lorran said, "We have several truckloads of lumber and materials on the way from Nairobi right now. They should be arriving next week. Also, I have a team of builders, craftsmen, and brickmasons who will be arriving next week to start construction. I need you and McKenzie to have Angel and his workers set up a cook station to feed the workers. I also will need about twenty of your workers to help. Do you think you can handle that part on your end?"

Wallace said, "I'm sure I can."

Lorran said, "I'm going to leave my plane here. One of my friends from Nairobi is flying down here to pick me up and fly us to Cairo, Egypt. We will be picking up the 1930 Stinson trimotor plane we just bought to transport our new clients." Lorran called McKenzie and asked her to bring some wine glasses out. "I have a bottle of French champagne that I have been saving for this occasion in my plane. Rowan, will you please run down and get it for me?" After a toast to Eden's future safari camp, McKenzie told everyone to come inside. She said she had prepared a meal fit for big game hunters. Wallace, Lorran, Rowan, and McKenzie talked into the night about their plans for their new adventure.

The next morning, a couple of hours after sunup, Lorran's friend flew into Eden's airstrip, picked up Lorran, and started their journey to Cairo, Egypt, to pick up the new plane.

McKenzie said, "Tomorrow is Sunday, why don't we drive up to the mission at Ngorongoro? I received a letter from Mrs. Sharp. She said they had a new visitor that she would like us to meet, especially Rowan." They all boarded on one of the trucks early the next morning. Angel had heard they were going and insisted that he get to go also where he could see his old friends, the Sharps. When the Leslies arrived at the mission, they were met by the Sharps, their congregation, and a beautiful young Danish girl by the name of Angela.

As soon as Rowan's and Angela's eyes met, he was hooked. Mrs. Sharp said, "Come on in and have some refreshments, church will begin in about one hour." Angela was not shy; she walked right over and spoke to Rowan. Rowan was speechless, living in the bush most of his life, he was really without words. He had no idea what this beautiful woman might want to talk about. He knew plenty about the bush and the animals that lived there. He had not ever talked very much to any White female except his mom and Ladan, which no one knew anything about, and Ladan was more about action and less about talking.

Angela asked Rowan to tell her about himself, how long he had lived in Africa, what he liked to do, if he did play sports, what his favorite food was, and if he traveled much. One thing Rowan knew was that Angela was very beautiful; she was tall, probably five feet ten, and with beautiful blond hair, which she wore in a long French braid. She had the bluest eyes he had ever seen. She had a German or Danish accent and was very well-spoken. He could tell she was well educated.

Rowan said, "Tell me something about you!"

Angela said, "I'm an orphan and was raised in an orphanage in Copenhagen. When I turned sixteen, I joined a mission team, and my first assignment is here at Ngorongoro. The Sharps are so nice, and I love the people here in Africa so much. I'm going to ask my supervisor if I can live here and help for several years at this mission."

Rowan said, "That is so great, there are not any Europeans that live in this part of Africa, and I don't know one White person my age that lives anywhere near here. It will be great if you do stay. Our farm is not that far away, and I would love to have you for a friend."

Angela said, "I would love to be friends with you, Rowan. I will get the Sharps to drive us over soon and visit with you and your family."

Mrs. Sharp called Rowan and Angela in for the morning church service. After the service, Mrs. Sharp invited the Leslies to their house for lunch with tea and cookies later. After lunch, Rowan and Angela sat on the porch swing and talked. Rowan told Angela about his life in Africa, and she told him about her life in Denmark. They chatted all afternoon.

Wallace said, "Okay, you, two, we are going to have to go to make it back to the farm before night." Angela hugged Rowan and promised she would visit the farm soon. As the Leslies were returning home, Wallace, McKenzie, and Emma rode in front of the truck, and Angel and Rowan were in the back. McKenzie said to Wallace, "Do you hear Rowan singing in the back of the truck? She replied that Rowan never sings. Wallace said, "He is a young man, and beautiful young women have that effect on young men. I know you had that effect on me."

McKenzie said, "I think you were more lovestruck than Rowan is."

Wallace said, "You are right about that."

They arrived home right at sunset. Rowan stuck his head in through the sliding back glass of the truck and said, "Mom, is that not the most beautiful sunset you have ever seen?"

McKenzie looked at Wallace and said, "You are right, Rowan is lovestruck."

The next day around 10:00 a.m., two more trucks pulled in, and Wallace, Rowan, and the workers started to unload the trucks. They were almost through unloading the trucks when they saw Dr. Finley's plane come in for a landing. Rowan saw Dr. Finley waving his hat in a come-here motion. Wallace and Rowan jumped off the back of the supply truck and ran up to the plane. Dr. Finley said Dr. Ross had called him and said Dr. Dunn had taken a turn for the worst and was asking for McKenzie to come to the hospital immediately. Wallace told Rowan to run and tell his mom to come immediately and for him to stay with his sister. Rowan did as he was told. McKenzie came running to the plane, and she said, "What should I do?"

Wallace said, "Go with Dr. Finley, Lorran is supposed to be here anytime in his new plane. We will get him to fly us onto Dar es Salaam as soon as he gets here. McKenzie, go on now, we will be okay."

About one hour later, Lorran landed at the airstrip. Rowan was amazed at the new plane; it was the largest plane he had ever seen. Wallace informed Lorran what had happened to Dr. Dunn. Lorran told Wallace, "As soon as we can refuel the plane, I will fly you and Rowan onto the hospital." It took about thirty minutes to pump a fifty-gallon tank of fuel into the plane, and Lorran, Wallace, Emma, and Rowan were on their way to Dar es Salaam.

When they arrived, they caught a cab and rushed to the hospital. Ladan met them at the front door and said, "It is not good! He took a turn for the worse last night." When they reached the room, McKenzie was outside the door. She was crying. "The doctor said he didn't have much time left. "Let me take Emma in, and Dad wants to see you, Wallace, alone. Then, he wants to see Rowan alone also."

When Rowan walked in the room, he could hardly recognize his grandfather; his skin was yellow, and his body was frail. He held out his hand and said, "Rowan, come close and let me hold your hand." He continued, "Rowan, you are my only grandson, and you are the very sunshine of each day of my life since the day you were born. You have grown into a young man whom I'm so proud of. If I could pick any young man in this whole world to be my grandson, it would be you. I'm so proud of you, you have brought happiness and joy to each day of my life, and I thank God for giving you and McKenzie to me. Take care of your mom and little sister. Rowan, I ask one thing of you, when I pass on to be with God, please you and your dad bury me on the hill behind the landing strip where we used to sit and watch the sunset through the acacia trees. There is a little rise where we have seen the big male lion sometimes lay and watch the sun setting. Do you know where I am talking about?"

Rowan said, "Yes, we have seen the big male lion lay on the little rise before as the sun sets."

Dr. Dunn said, "Please, bury me there, and please dig the grave deep and then lay flat stones from the creek on my grave."

Rowan said, "I will, Granddad."

Dr. Dunn said, "You know I don't want any hyenas digging my old bones up."

Rowan said, "Do not worry, Grandfather, don't worry, and I want you to know, I will see you again soon on the other side, and we will take another walkabout through the Serengeti." Dr. Dunn passed on to the other side later that night. The next day, Dr. Finley and Wallace placed Dr. Dunn in the back seat of his plane and flew back to Eden for the last time. Lorran, Ladan, Wallace, McKenzie, Rowan, and Emma flew back in Lorran's plane.

When they arrived at Eden, they placed Dr. Dunn at the main house where all of the Hadzabe people, Maasai, and his friends could come by and pay their respect to the family.

Rowan, Jian, Kasi, and Khufu dug the grave for Dr. Dunn; they dug it twice the depth of a normal grave, and after the service, they placed large flat stones from the creek on top of the grave. Ladan came over and hugged Rowan, but it was different this time; she had tears in her eyes. She had visited Dr. Dunn every day at the hospital and would take a basket of fruit and a little rum flask. She told Rowan that the time she got to spend with Dr. Dunn was special, and he was a special man.

The Sharps had come to the funeral and had brought Angela with them. Rowan was sad and felt lost without his granddad. He had walked down to the coffee warehouse and was sitting on a bag of coffee when Angela walked up and put her arm around Rowan. She said, "I'm so sorry I never got to meet your granddad, but I can tell how close you two were." Angela pulled Rowan closer and kissed him on the cheek. When she did, Rowan slowly pushed her back onto the coffee bean sack and kissed her on the lips. She slapped him and said, "I'm not that kind of girl." Rowan was confused and hurt from just losing his granddad. The only woman he had ever kissed before was Ladan, and now, he had kissed Angela, and she had thrown him in a curveball. What should he do, Rowan kissed her again. This time, she slapped him even harder, so he slapped her back and said, "You don't know how to kiss anyway!" Angela jumped off the coffee bag and ran back to the main house crying. Later that afternoon, Rowan apologized to Angela and said, "I know I'm a man, and I am sorry. I have just never been around a girl in my whole life, and I just don't know how European girls and women think. When you kissed me, I thought you wanted me to kiss you back."

Angela said, "I did want you to kiss me."

Rowan said, "Why did you slap me then?"

She said, "I was defending my honor."

Rowan said, "Angela, I really like you, but I just don't understand the way you think about kissing. Maybe we just need to sit down one day and discuss this subject in deep detail." Rowan and Angela shook hands and agreed they were still friends and liked each other. They planned on having a picnic next Sunday after church.

The following day, the construction crew began working on the lodge and the camp storage warehouse. It took a little over two weeks to complete the lodge and warehouse. The lodge had electricity, which was powered by a generator and running water. The pump was powered by a water ram located near the spring where there was a large water tank. Lorran had the builders build a nice rock and wood cottage close to the spring for him and Ladan to live while they would be staying at Eden.

All of Lorran and Wallace's plans had come together without any real problems. The craftsmen from Nairobi and Arusha had worked well with the workers from the coffee operation on the farm. Lorran and Wallace thanked the workers for completing the job ahead of schedule.

Lorran told Wallace that he was worried because he had a guest scheduled to arrive the following Monday to start a hunting safari and another group of guests arriving Tuesday to start a photo safari. He said, "I don't know what we would have done if the craftsmen had not finished the lodge."

Wallace said, "I guess we would have had to put them up in our house."

Lorran asked Wallace if it would be okay for Rowan, Khufu, and Jian to lead the photo safari, and he would take Elias and Kasi with him on the hunting safari. Wallace said, "Yes, I think it will be good for Rowan. It should give him a feeling of ownership and strengthen his leadership skills. You and Rowan are going to have to be responsible for the safari operations, my and McKenzie's main concern is the coffee production, and it requires our full attention most of the time."

Lorran said, "I have three crews working on the three campsites right now. If it's okay, I'm going to take Rowan with me and check out the sites and make sure they will be ready for guests next week. We will have our camp at Lake Eyasi and two in the Serengeti, one permanent camp and one mobile camp, so we can follow the migration in vehicles." Lorran told Wallace that when the workers were through building the permanent camps, he would like Wallace to send some of the workers from the farm to build landing strips at Lake Eyasi and at the permanent campsite in the Serengeti.

Wallace said, "That will be no problem, most of the men at the farm have some spare time this time of year."

Lorran told Wallace that he, Rowan, and Elias were going to take one of the farm trucks with some extra supplies out to the campsites and check on the workers' progress.

Saturday afternoon, Lorran and Rowan returned and reported that the camps were up and functional. Lorran told Wallace and Rowan that he was going to fly to Dar es Salaam and pick up the guests who would be on the photo safari for Tuesday. "I will be back with that group Sunday afternoon, they are in Nairobi. Then, Monday, Elias and I will lead the hunters to camp one in the Serengeti, and Rowan can take his guests to the camp at Lake Eyasi for a couple of days, then he can move his quests on up to the mobile safari in the Serengeti."

Wallace told Lorran he needed to get some rest and said, "You and Rowan have a busy week ahead of you."

The next morning, Lorran flew to Dar es Salaam and picked up two hunters, and he brought Ladan back with him for her to check out her new part-time home at Eden. Shortly, after he arrived, he had the plane refueled and flew to Nairobi to pick up the other guests.

The next morning, Lorran took one truck and one touring vehicle with him. Lorran, Ladan, the two hunters, Elias, and Kasi headed to the hunting camp in the Serengeti.

The two hunters were John East and Robert Bullard, both experienced hunters from London, England. Both of them had made their fortunes in naval shipping. When they arrived at the camp, they were met by the camp manager chief and camp personnel. The camp setup was very elegant but also very rugged and had an African safari personal touch to it.

That night at dinner, the chef presented a feast fit for royalty: prime ribs, Caesar salad, freshly baked bread, fresh vegetables, vintage wine, and a delicious dark chocolate cake with walnuts and a scoop of vanilla rum ice cream and chocolate syrup drizzled on it. Robert Bullard commented, "You cannot get food like this even back in the most exclusive restaurants in London or Paris." After dinner, they all sat around the campfire that the staff had prepared. As they sipped some scotch whiskey, Lorran shared with them the plan of tomorrow's hunt. Both hunters wanted to kill a trophy African lion. They both have agreed to Lorran's price if he could deliver on their goal. As they sat and talked, Ladan noticed Mr. East staring at her. She had been around enough drunk men to know what was on his mind.

She said, "Gentlemen, if you will please excuse me, I'm going to retire for tonight." She ran her fingers through Lorran's hair, and he said, "Excuse me, gentlemen, I will see you at daybreak in the morning. Be ready for the most exciting day of your life."

At daybreak, Elias woke the two hunters up and informed them that breakfast was ready. After breakfast, Elias and Kasi left the camp in search of two large male lions they had seen on the previous hunting trip to the area. When the two hunters and Lorran finished their breakfast, they left the camp following the small white cloth flags that Elias had left for them to follow. After they had traveled about four kilometers, they saw Elias and Kasi returning. Lorran could tell that Elias was very upset, and when he reached them, Lorran said, "What is the matter, Elias?" Elias stuck his spear into the ground and said, "Damn poachers." Elias was a hunter and killed only when he or his family needed food. He loved Africa and respected nature and cared for the animals. He often referred to the animals as his family; a gift and wonder given to the earth from God.

Chapter 14

The Poachers

Elias told Lorran and the hunters that some poachers had killed a whole herd of elephants, big bulls, cows, and even calves. He said, "My heart cries with sadness, there is no excuse for killing a whole family of elephants. I hate poachers, and they must pay for their sin against Africa and against God."

Lorran said, "I will help you find them and bring them to justice."

Elias said, "No, this is my home, the killers are Africans. Kasi and I will avenge the elephants' deaths." Elias pulled his spear out of the ground, and he and Kasi ran toward the east, leaving the hunters and Lorran standing alone. Mr. Bullard said, "Do we need them to guide us?"

Lorran said, "Yes. I would not face two large male lions alone without Elias. I have seen him kill a leopard and a lion with his spear, he has no fear, and he knows the animals here on the Serengeti like his own brothers."

Mr. East said, "Are we safe with Elias, he seems pretty well unhinged about the killing of the elephants."

Lorran said, "No worry, I trust Elias with my life, and when it comes the time to kill the two lions, he will be right by your side. What the poachers did to the elephant family is unacceptable, and they will pay dearly if Elias and Kasi find them."

Lorran and the two hunters followed their trail back to the camp. Lorran apologized and said, "If Elias returns this afternoon, we will hunt the lions tomorrow." Just as the sun was setting, Elias and Kasi returned to camp, Kasi had a bad cut on his left arm where someone had cut him with a machete. Ladan and Lorran took him in the dining tent and laid him on one of the dining tables. Lorran took some whiskey and cleaned his wound. He told Ladan to find a needle and thread. She returned, and he started to sew up the deep cut. Ladan was the first to notice the necklace that Kasi and Elias had around their necks. It was a piece of long rawhide with some pieces of flesh that were on the string like ornaments on the rawhide. Ladan said, "Elias, what is that you and Kasi have on your necklace?"

Elias responded, "It is the ears of the poachers. They will not kill any more elephants." Ladan felt dizzy, and the next thing she knew, she was lying on one of the tables in the dining room; she had fainted. After finishing sewing Kasi's arm up, Lorran asked Elias to tell them what had happened. Elias explained that they had found the poachers. They were Somali poachers, and they had a camp inside of a large hollow baobab tree. Elias said, "There were six of them, and they were all drunk and sleeping. Kasi and I quietly and slowly killed each of them, the last one that Kasi killed cut him with a machete."

Lorran said, "What about the bodies, what did you do with them?"

Elias said, "The hyenas were hungry, you know, all of God's creatures have to eat." Ladan clutched Lorran's hand, and she felt like she was going to faint again.

Elias told Lorran that the poachers had a large stash of ivory hidden in the large hollow baobab tree. He said, "Since Kasi and I found the ivory and killed the poachers, I believe that we should get at least half of it. You and Wallace can have the other half, there is no reason to let the ivory go to waste. The elephants gave their lives for it."

Lorran said, "Elias, we will go with you and collect the ivory, and we will sell it for our operation could use the extra money, for we have a lot of payments coming due at the end of the year."

The next morning, Elias led the two hunters and Lorran out on the Serengeti in search of two large male lions, while Kasi and several of the camp crew took one of the trucks and traveled to the large hollow baobab tree to recover the ivory.

After walking about two hours, Elias found the large male lion feasting on a kudu antelope they had killed. Elias had never liked killing when it was not necessary, but he had led hunts for the Meyer brothers, and he knew it was the coming way of life in Africa. He told Lorran and the hunters to walk around the feeding lions and get on the south side of them where they could not pick up their scent since the wind was blowing from the north. When the hunters got positioned for their shots, Lorran told East to take the lion on the left and Bullard to take the lion on the right. He said, "If the first shot does not kill the lion, fire again and reload. Elias and I will cover you, and we will shoot if you feel you are in trouble." Elias had a gun and also was carrying his spear and shield.

Elias yelled at the lion and beat his spear against his shield; the lion on the left charged. Mr. East fired and missed. He fired again and hit the lion on the left-back leg; it continued to charge. Lorran shot twice hitting the lion in the chest, it flipped and lay dead. The other lion started to charge, then it turned and started to run into the bushes. Mr. Bullard shot it, but the bullet hit the lion in the stomach. It turned and started running toward the hunters. Mr. Bullard turned and started to run away. Lorran had reloaded by now and shot the lion on the left shoulder and then shot it in the heart. Both lions lay dead; everyone was pretty shaken up. Mr. East said, "I did not realize how fast one of those big lions could move."

Mr. Bullard said, "I'm sorry, guys. I don't know why I ran."

Lorran said, "That happens sometimes with a new hunter. You will do better next time." Elias and Lorran started to skin the lions. Lorran told Mr. East that he would have the lion's skin cleaned and tanned and get a taxidermist in Dar es Salaam to mount the lions and have them sent to London if they would like that. Mr. East said he would like to use the skin for a rug for his study. Mr. Bullard said, "I would like to do the same with mine." Lorran told them what the cost was for the taxidermist to tan the hides of the two lions, and both men agreed that the cost was fair. Lorran said, "We will pack the hides in salt, and I will fly them to Dar es Salaam for you where the taxidermist lives."

That night at dinner, all Mr. East and Mr. Bullard talked about was how Lorran had saved both of their lives and could not wait to tell their friends about the lion hunt. They assured Lorran they would send all of their friends who loved to hunt to his safari company.

The next day, the hunters would try their luck at killing a couple of large eland antelopes, which are as large as a cow, and they have magnificent horns. As the hunters were getting ready to leave on the walking safari, Elias and Kasi walked up to where they were eating breakfast under a large open tent. When Ladan saw the ear trophy that Elias and Kasi had around their neck, she gasped and ran into her tent feeling weak in her stomach.

Elias and Kasi headed out of the camp leaving a trail of white string flags as they moved to the west. Kasi had seen some eland close to a watering hole a couple of days earlier. As the hunters got ready to leave, Lorran kissed Ladan and said Rowan and his clients may stop by the camp sometime today. They have been at the camp at Lake Eyasi and would be moving to the mobile camp north of them in the Serengeti. Ladan asked Lorran if she could go on the photo safari. She told him she was bored just sitting at camp all day while he led the hunting party. He said, "I understand, you will probably have more fun actually following the migration by vehicle with Rowan than sitting here all day alone."

Rowan and his clients arrived at lunchtime at the second base camp where Ladan was. They were greeted by the camp staff, and all were given a fresh, refreshing fruit punch drink, and afterward, they had a good lunch. Ladan told Rowan that she had asked Lorran if she could travel with him to the third mobile camp in the Serengeti. Rowan said, "I thought you would want to stay here with Lorran, this is a very romantic setting here with the camp situated under the grove of acacia trees."

She said, "It is beautiful, but the only time I see Lorran is very early in the morning and very late at night, and I'm tired of sitting here all day with nothing to do but read safari novels written by some boring old hunters." After lunch, Rowan, Ladan, and the photo safari clients loaded back into the truck and the safari touring vehicle and headed north toward the mobile safari camp. When they reached the camp, it was almost sundown. The tents were located near a stream with acacia trees dotting the horizon. They were greeted by the camp staff and had a really great dinner.

After dinner, Rowan, Ladan, and the clients sat around the open campfire. Rowan introduced the guests to Ladan. He said, "This lady is Azniv Krikorian, she is from Armenia, she fled Armenia when the Armenians were slaughtered by the Ottoman Turks. Her original home was Constantinople, her family fled to Los Angeles, California, where her family bought a hotel near the coastline. This lady is her daughter, Mary Krikorian. Mary has cancer, and this has been her one wish to visit Africa. Aznar mortgaged her hotel to get the money for this safari, just where Mary would be able to fulfill her special dream.

"And this young lady is Taylor Krikorian, she belongs to Azniv's son, Ararat, and her mother is Lian Krikorvian, Lian is Japanese. This gentleman is Bob Kuralt, he is a professional photographer, he works for some of the most prestigious wildlife photo publishing companies in the United States and lives near Tucson, Arizona. And last, this is my good friend, Ladan Abdi, she lives in Dar es Salaam with Lorran, who you will meet later back at the lodge at Eden."

The next morning, after breakfast, the groups divided into two and took two vehicles out in the Serengeti to witness the great migration—the most spectacular movement of millions of animals from the Serengeti to the Maasai Mara to find fresh new grass as the weather pattern changes, and the rainfall moves more to the north.

The animals followed the rain looking for water and green grasses. Rowan stopped the vehicle at a large stone kopjes; there was a large male lion lying on one of the large rocks watching as the wildebeest and zebras passed by. He looked like a great king overlooking his kingdom and his subjects. Ladan looked over at Mary, and she saw tears running down her face. Ladan put her arm around Mary, and they both cried together. Mary said, "Ever since I was a little girl, I have dreamed of visiting Africa. Africa is the only place I have ever wanted to visit, and now, I am here. I am so thankful to God for granting me my wish," but she continued, "I'm not ready to die. I am still a young woman. I'm only thirty-five." Ladan pulled her close, and they both cried together. Everyone was quiet and silent; they knew this was a sad moment but also a happy and fulfilling time for Mary. She soon would go home to be with her creator who had blessed her with the wish of witnessing His greatest creations—the great migration in the Serengeti.

The big lion got up and disappeared back into the large rocks of the kopjes. Rowan drove north, and they reached the Mara River. Thousands of wildebeests and zebras were crossing the river heading up into the Maasai Mara searching for fresh green grass. Rowan pointed out the large crocodiles, which were as large as the vehicles. They were snatching and devouring the wildebeest and zebras as they crossed the river. Mary and Ladan turned their heads and looked away. Rowan said the crocodiles caught a few of the animals as they were crossing, but many more were trampled or drowned by the large flood of animals crossing at one time. The large crocodiles feast for months on the carcass until the herds move back south to the Serengeti, crossing the Mara River again.

As they were driving back to the camp, Ladan was sitting next to Taylor. She asked Taylor how old she was. She said, "I am twelve years old."

And Ladan said, "Do you know, you are a very beautiful young lady."

Taylor replied, "That's what my parents tell me. I know all the boys at school want me to be their girlfriend, but I'm not really interested in boys. I'm more into sports. I love soccer." Taylor told Ladan,

"You are very beautiful too, you know, I wish I could live here in Africa like you do."

Ladan replied, "Follow your dreams and come back to Africa when you finish school, I would love for you to live here and be my friend."

The little group arrived back at camp to a very good dinner waiting on them. After dinner, Rowan sat down on a large stone next to the firepit and was watching the sunset through the acacia grove. When Ladan came over and sat down next to him and handed him a glass of wine, she said, "Rowan, we are two blessed people to see a sunset like that here in this beautiful land we call Africa."

He said, "Yes, we are, I would not trade lives with anyone, not even the king of England."

Ladan said, "I would not either." She reached over and took his hand into hers. She said, "Rowan, you are my most special friend, and I enjoy being with you so much."

Rowan said, "I really like you, Ladan, and you are my best friend. You understand me better than anyone else. You really have to be born and raised in Africa to understand someone who was born here."

Ladan said, "That is true." The rest of the guests circled around the firepit. The cook brought a tray of wine, tea, coffee, and hot chocolate to the firepit. Another cook brought some fresh cookies and some popcorn. Rowan, Ladan, and the guests sat around the fire and shared stories into the night. Finally, Rowan said, "We have a busy day planned tomorrow, we all need to get some sleep."

Rowan went to his tent, and Ladan went to her tent. Rowan thought Ladan had probably gone to sleep; she had not shown him any attention since his last night with her at the villa at Dar es Salaam. He was starting to drift off into a deep sleep when he heard someone unzip his tent. He raised up and saw it was Ladan entering his tent. She lay down beside him, and he started to kiss the back of her neck. She said, "Rowan, I don't want to make love to you tonight. I just want you to put your arms around me and hold me, hold me tight." Rowan put his arms around her and pulled her close to himself so he could smell the sweet fragrance of her perfume"

He remembered the smell of the fragrance from the night at the villa. When he held the pillow she lay on, he pulled her closer and tried to burn the thought of the moment into his mind forever. Ladan said, "Rowan, you are my best friend, and I love being with you more than anyone else I know. I love Lorran, but I enjoy being with you more." She slowly drifted off to sleep, but Rowan couldn't forget the last time they had slept together. He started to caress her legs. She said, "Please just hold me and go to sleep." Rowan finally drifted into a deep sleep, and when he woke up, Ladan was gone. He could smell her fragrance in his bed, and he wished she would have stayed longer.

The cook woke everyone up early for breakfast. Rowan walked to the dining tent and sat down. Ladan walked up and ran her hand through his hair and said, "How did you sleep last night?"

He said, "I slept very little. I had a very beautiful woman who made a visit to my tent last night."

Ladan said, "It was one of the African girls. I bet it was that tall beautiful one who was always staring at you. The cook's assistant who always brought you cookies and hot chocolate."

Rowan responded, "Yes, it's one of the African girls, and she also is my best friend."

Rowan, Ladan, Mary, and Taylor loaded into one of the touring vehicles and started their day on the safari. They drove to a large lake and saw thousands of flamingos and passed a flock of ostriches. They stopped at the water hole for lunch and were serenaded by a large herd of elephants swimming in the water. The baby elephants were having so much fun that Ladan wondered how anyone could kill these magnificent creatures. She thought of the necklace that Elias and Kasi were wearing with the ears of the poachers. She had a change of heart, and she said to herself, *I would do just like Elias did and cut the poachers' ears off if I had seen them killing those sweet baby elephants.* A group of baboons showed up, and Rowan had to quickly put up the food before the baboons could make off with it. None of the animals really had any fear of man. The White man was a new creature in their world, and they had not learned to fear him yet, but they soon would learn how cruel and evil the White man can be.

As they were driving back to the camp, Taylor said, "What is that awful smell?"

Rowan responded, "There is a hyena's den nearby, I can smell them also."

Ladan said, "That smell is awful, let's get out of here before it makes me sick."

Rowan said, "There it is." He pulled closer, and several of the hyenas came out of the den.

Taylor said, "Those are horrid-looking creatures, and they smell so bad. They look like werewolves. I have seen them in horror films at the theater. Please, let's leave, I'm frightened."

Ladan said, "Rowan, please, let's go. Taylor, I'm going to have nightmares tonight, I know I will."

When they reached camp, they were greeted by Bob Kuralt. Bob was so excited. He said, "This is the best photo shoot I have been on. Khufu is the best guide in Africa. I have some photos here that I have taken that will be in the *National Geographic*. I'm sure before this year is over. This is a first-class operation that you are running here. One thing I like about it is that it is run by real Africans who know the layout of the land, the native people, and where all the animals are. I promise by this time next year, when I tell all my friends about your safari company, you will have so many people wanting to come to Eden. You will have to book your safari adventures two years in advance."

The next morning, Rowan, Ladan, and all the guests told the camp staff goodbye and headed back to Eden to pick up their next group of guests. This had been a real jewel of an adventure. Everyone had a fun time, Bob had got some award-winning photos, and many lifelong dreams had finally come true.

Taylor had found a true love where she would make her home someday in Africa. As they drove back, Mary looked at the vista of trees, kopjes, and thousands of different animals and birds. She closed her eyes and thanked God for the wonderful thirty-five years of her life, her family, and her mom who had sacrificed so much to make her dream come true. She thanked Him for this dream come true. She thanked Him for her new friends, and mostly, she thanked God for the most wonderful adventure we all call life. Ladan put her arms around Mary and said, "I love you, and I will be praying that God will heal you. Mary, I consider you as my friend, I hope you feel the same about me. I'm so glad that I was blessed to share this part of my life with such a wonderful woman and her family. I will never forget you, Mary."

Mary said, "I will never forget you, Ladan, and I will never forget the kindness and love that you and Rowan have shown me on this trip that I have dreamed of all my life. You have even made it more special."

When they arrived back at Eden, they were welcomed by McKenzie and Wallace. All of the guests were excited and told McKenzie that they loved her home, and they had the best safari ever and promise they all would return someday. They exchanged addresses and promised to write. Lorran arrived and told the photo safari group that they would be flying out within the hour. He told the hunters he would be back in the morning and get them back to the airport in Nairobi tomorrow in time to catch their flight back to London.

Ladan told Lorran she wanted to fly back to Dar es Salaam with him. She said she had fun, but she missed her home on the beach. She promised him she would go on another safari with him soon, but she was homesick for Dar es Salaam.

The passengers all loaded onto the plane and they flew out to Dar es Salaam. The next morning, Lorran returned to Eden with six more guests ready to start a photo safari. Rowan said, "Lorran, this last safari was fun, but this is like work, we only get one day off."

Lorran said, "That's how we grow a business and make money." Lorran helped Mr. East, and Mr. Bullard boarded the plane. Lorran had packed the cargo department and had all of the extra space in the cabin packed with the ivory they had taken from the poachers. The plane struggled as it took off; Lorran had put too much weight on the plane. He landed safely in Nairobi but told Mr. East and Mr. Bullard that he was a little worried about the takeoff and would never load the plane that heavy again. The hunters thanked Lorran and promised they would be back next year and would tell all of their friends about his safari company.

Lorran met his two new clients, Mr. Roy Willis and Jack Estes, also from England, and they headed to Eden to start their hunting safari. Lorran had done well in his planning for the safari lodge and safari camps. He had a list of clients booked for the next two months, and he had a friend in Nairobi who was handling the booking for him, and he had told Lorran that his phone rang constantly. Lorran had run a couple of ads in the newspapers and magazines in England and the United States one month before he and Wallace had opened the company, and the advertising had really paid off. He said to himself, *That was the best investment I had ever made.* Everyone was starting to travel more since World War I had ended, and the world was getting back to normal again. Lorran thought to himself, *I will be a millionaire before I'm fifty.* Not only was the safari service booming, so was the coffee plantation. Wallace had three bumper crops in a row, and coffee prices were at an all-time high. Angel had turned Eden coffee into one of the most sought-after coffees in Africa. Both Eden coffee and the safari business that Wallace and Lorran had developed were both doing extremely well. Wallace asked Lorran if he would have any problems if he sold his share of the safari service to Rowan. He said, "I don't have time to really fool with it anyway. I need to spend more time concentrating on the coffee, and Rowan is really running part of the safari business anyway."

Lorran said, "That would be great with me, Rowan and I work well together, and he has his heart and soul invested in the company anyway. I'm sure he could run the camps without me anyway. He still does not know much about the financial end of the business and the part about booking new clients." Wallace asked Lorran to meet with him and Rowan after dinner and discuss the transfer of responsibility to Rowan. After dinner that night, Lorran, Wallace, and Rowan sat down and drew up a business partnership contract. They all signed it, shook hands, and Lorran said, "I will give it to our lawyer and let him go over it, file, and make it legal. Rowan was so happy he was a half owner in the safari company that he loved so much.

Lorran kept new clients flowing in each week. Rowan told Lorran he liked the photography side of the business better than the hunting side and asked Lorran if he could just run that side of the business and Lorran could run the hunting side. Lorran said that was fine, and he would rather be out on a hunt than riding in a touring vehicle with a bunch of women, children, and birdwatchers anyway. Lorran hired a big game hunter out of South Africa from a hunting lodge to help him shuttle the hunters in and out of the camps.

Chapter 15

Death of Jian and Khufu

The big game hunter's name was Riks Becker. Rowan did not like Riks; he had a short temper and was hard on the African trackers. Elias did not like him either. He told Lorran, "Riks has no respect for the animals and kills them for no reason except fun." Lorran assured Rowan and Elias that he would fire Riks as soon as he could find another experienced hunter to replace him.

Rowan had taken a group out on a photo safari; one of the photographers was a Belgian aristocrat who had a much younger French wife. She was very beautiful and very flirty with Rowan. She would touch his arm or hair and say, "You are the most handsome man I have seen since we have been in Africa." Her husband, Carl Wilhelm, told Rowan not to pay any attention to her flirting; he said all French women are that way. Rowan was attracted to her, and he felt she was attracted to him. Her name was Danielle. She was always sitting next to Rowan in the vehicle or when they were having dinner. When no one was looking, she would rub her foot against Rowan's leg; this was starting to arouse Rowan's interest. One night after dinner, everyone was sitting around the campfire, and it was getting late. Carl and his new safari friend Kyle Hall were discussing birds they had photographed that day. Rowan said, "Please excuse me, I have some business to take care of with the camp manager, and I'm going to turn in for the night." After discussing tomorrow's agenda with the camp manager, he went to his tent, unzipped the tent, and to his surprise,

Danielle was lying in his bunk. She reached up and grabbed his hand and pulled Rowan onto the bed and passionately kissed his lips and neck. Danielle said, "Have you ever made love to a French woman?"

Rowan responded, "I have made love to a woman that was half French." She said that would do and pulled him into the bed with her. He asked Danielle, "What about Carl?" She said he would talk all night to his new friend and that he was too old to make love anyway. As soon as Danielle was through with Rowan, she went to her tent. Carl was still sitting at the fire talking to his friend Kyle. Rowan just lay in his bed. He said, "I have the best job in the world. I would not trade jobs with the king of England."

The next day, Rowan had taken his clients to a water hole, and they were having lunch, while Carl and Kyle photographed a herd of elephants that were playing in the water. Kasi pulled up in one of the safari vehicles and said, "Rowan, come quick! Khufu and Jina have been hurt very badly." Rowan asked the tracker with him to guide the clients back to camp, and he asked Carl if he could drive the vehicle, and Carl said sure.

When Kasi and Rowan reached the site where Khufu and Jian were, they could see a large drove of vultures feeding. Kasi said, "No, that's where I left Khufu and Jian." As they approached the site, several hyenas ran away. Rowan fired his pistol into the air, and vultures flew away, leaving only pieces of the two men's bodies. Kasi started to cry, and he said that was Khufu and Jian. Rowan dropped to his knees and said, "What happened?"

Kasi said, "We were guiding for a White hunter, he wanted to kill a big bull elephant. When he fired, he missed his mark and hit the elephant in the front leg, and it charged, killing the hunter. Then, it charged Riks, he shot and killed the elephant and started shooting all the elephants in the herd. Jian and Khufu tried to stop him, and he shot them both and then started firing at me, and I ran to Elias. Elias was hunting with another hunter, and I told him. He told me to get you, and then he went after Riks."

Rowan asked Kasi, "where is Lorran, go and tell him to come here immediately, tell him to send the hunter that was with him back to camp, don't let the other hunters know what happened here."

Just as Kasi and Lorran reached the spot where Rowan was, Elias appeared out of the bushes covered in blood. Lorran asked Elias if he was okay. Elias came and fell down on the ground next to Jian and Khufu and started making these strange moaning sounds. He beat the ground with his large fist. Then, he stood up and said, "If you were not my friends and family, I would kill both of you right now. I told both of you Riks was bad, I asked you to get rid of him, now look what he has done. He has killed my oldest son Jian and my friend's son Khufu. Why didn't you just listen to me? If you had, this would have not happened." He looked at Lorran and drew his spear back and said, "The only thing that means anything to you is money, more money, more money."

Rowan said, "Elias, where is Riks?"

Elias responded, "He is in hell."

"Where is Riks's body?"

Elias said it was in the belly of a hyena. Rowan and Lorran loaded up the bodies of the White hunter, Jian, and Khufu and headed back to Eden.

Lorran canceled the two safaris that were going on and took everyone back to Eden for the funerals and burial of Jian and Khufu. Rowan packed the White hunter's body in salt and placed him in a coffin and shipped him back to England. Rowan and Lorran decided to cancel the next safaris scheduled for the following week. Lorran had a friend who had a safari service that he ran out of Arusha. He agreed to pick up the two groups of people whose safari had been canceled and took them on a safari using his company out of Arusha. Lorran refunded both groups; their full deposits on the Safari trips he had canceled.

Everyone at Eden was totally devastated. Rowan and Lorran knew that news would spread about the disaster that their company had experienced. They wondered if their company would survive. No one had seen Elias since Jian and Khufu were killed. Rowan said, "I'm sure he is out there somewhere in the Serengeti. I just hope he is okay and doesn't get distracted and let his guard down and do something foolish."

The next week, everyone just took a breather. Lorran flew to Dar es Salaam and picked Ladan up and brought her back to Eden. The Sharps came to visit and brought Angela. Rowan and Angela sat and talked for hours about life, how short it could be, and how fragile and precious it is. The week passed slowly, which gave everyone time to reflect on what had happened on the last safari.

Lorran said, "We got eight clients coming in Monday, is everyone up to it?"

Wallace said, "It's best if we don't dwell on our losses for too long. It will be best for everyone if we continue on Monday, just like it's another day for the Africa safari. The safari waits on no one."

Lorran picked up the guests in Dar es Salaam and Nairobi. It took him all day to make the two trips. Monday evening, just as everyone was finishing dinner, Elias walked up to the dining room at the lodge. He had his third oldest son, Jola, and Kasi with him. He looked at Lorran and said, "I'm at peace with you, my friend. My two sons and I will be here at daybreak to help you and Rowan guide the hunters." It was like a mountain had been lifted from Lorran's back. He was happy that Elias had forgiven him and was back to help.

Chapter 16

World War II

Everything ran smoothly at the plantation and the safari service until September of 1939 when World War II broke out. Shortly after the war started, clients started canceling their safari booking dates. Lorran's business partners started putting pressure on him, wanting the payments that he and Rowan were behind on. Then, in November, Rowan received a notice from the British Selective Service Department telling him to report Dar es Salaam for a military evaluation. The officer who interviewed him told him that he needed to go home and get everything in order because he would probably be called into service in the next couple of weeks. Two weeks later, he received a letter telling him to report to the British military base at Dar es Salaam. McKenzie was very upset and cried all night. Rowan assured her that if he could survive in the African bush all these years, surely, he would be okay in the Army. Wallace told McKenzie that no one knew how to survive any better than Rowan. Lorran told Rowan he would fly him to Dar es Salaam, but he would not be able to stay for he had a meeting with a banker in Nairobi. Lorran's investors were demanding payment, and Lorran would have to find someone to finance the plane, vehicles, and camp house, or he would lose them all. Lorran dropped Rowan off at the airport in Dar es Salaam and told him to catch a cab to the villa. He said, "Ladan is there, just make yourself at home, and I will try to get back and see you before you ship out."

Rowan caught a cab. When he arrived at the villa, he saw Ladan sitting on the beach. He walked down to where she was sitting and pulled up a lawn chair. Ladan said," I heard you are going to be leaving me. Do you know that I will miss you so very much? Rowan, I have watched you grow from a boy into a brave, handsome young man who is my very best friend."

Rowan said, "Ladan, you are my best friend also." Ladan asked Rowan where Lorran was. Rowan said he dropped him off at the airport and flew on to Nairobi to try and get a loan from a bank to keep the safari service going.

Ladan said, "The safari service is dead, and it will take everything Lorran has ever worked for, he is going to lose everything. The planes, the vehicles, the lodge, and my home here, my beautiful home that I love so much. Did you know he is going to mortgage the villa today to try to save his silly safari company? I don't know where I will go or what I will do if he loses my home."

Rowan said, "You can always come to Eden and live with us. My mom and dad love you, and you know I love you too."

A tear rolled down Ladan's cheek. She said, "Rowan, I love you too, I always have from the very first time I saw you. I was drawn to you like I have never been drawn to any other man, not even Lorran. The reason I have stayed with Lorran is because of all the fine things in life he has given me, and I know he loves me in his own way, but he loves money and power more than he loves me or you or Eden. He's a good man, and I accept all of his flaws because he is good to me, he always has been." Ladan asked, "Are you hungry? Come on up to the house, and I will fix you one of my special French dishes." After dinner, Ladan told Rowan to come with her. She led him down to the ocean. She dropped her le pagne on the sand of the beach and waded in the warm ocean water. She said, "Are you going to come in the water, or are you just going to watch?" Rowan undressed quickly and joined Ladan in the dark moonlit water. She pulled him close and said, "Slowly, slowly." She slowly kissed his lips, and he pulled her close and his hands slowly caressing her soft, olive skin. Rowan felt like he had been transported to the dream world. He remembered so well when he first visited years ago when he first kissed Ladan.

Ladan took his hand and led him back toward the villa. She stopped and picked up her skirt. Rowan grabbed his shirt and trousers. Ladan led him to the guest bedroom where they spent the rest of the night.

The next day, Rowan reported to the military base. They told him he would be shipping out first thing tomorrow morning. They told him to be there by 6:00 a.m., or he will be considered AWOL. The officer told him that he would ship out with the rest of the African troops to England where he would undergo military training.

Rowan was very sad; he loved Africa, and he loved Ladan. He did not want to leave his two loves, but he knew he must serve his country. His dad and grandfather had served, and he did not want to bring dishonor to them or his family. Rowan went back to the villa. Ladan and Rowan held each other, and they both cried. Rowan said, "I don't want to leave, you are my family. Why do countries have to fight, why can't they just leave Africa out of the war?" Ladan and Rowan never left each other's side the rest of the evening or night.

Rowan woke up early and kissed Ladan's forehead and said, "I love you!"

Ladan said, "Please promise me that you will come back to me."

Rowan asked Ladan, "Will you marry me?"

Ladan said, "Come back to me, and I will marry you. I promise, Rowan, I will marry you." Rowan left for the army base, boarded a ship, and started his journey to England.

Rowan arrived at the port of New Forest in Southern England, and he and the rest of the African recruits were shipped to Blandford army base to begin their military training. Most of the recruits stationed there were from countries where Great Britain had colonies. Rowan would be in the Eleventh African Army Division, which was made up of troops from East and West Africa. Rowan fit right in with most of these young African recruits; most of them had grown up in an environment much like his. It did not take long for Rowan to make many new friends. Rowan missed his home in Africa. England was much different, and the people were different. Most of the British looked down on the Africa troop as lower-class savages.

Rowan's best friend was from Kenya; he had lived on a coffee plantation and had loved to hunt in the Maasai Mara in Kenya. Rowan would write to his mom, Angela, and Ladan every week.

After three months of training, Rowan got a word that his company would be sent to the front line in Belgium. He wrote to his mom, Mary, and Ladan and promised he would write every chance he got, but he did not know how often the mail would get through. He assured them that he was in good company and all of his friends were African boys who were skilled hunters and marksmen. Rowan said that the warfare on the Belgium front line would not be much different from hunting in the savannas of Africa.

Lorran and Ladan made a visit to Eden to talk about the safari company with Wallace and McKenzie. When they arrived, McKenzie noticed that Ladan was showing. McKenzie said, "I don't mean to pry, but are you expecting?"

Ladan said, "Yes, I'm a little over three months pregnant."

McKenzie said, "I'm so happy for you and Lorran, you deserve a change of fortune and some happiness." Ladan thanked McKenzie. After dinner, Lorran told Wallace and McKenzie that he would like to discuss the safari company's future with them.

Lorran said, "You know I put everything that Ladan and I had into this venture. I even mortgaged our villa in Das es Salaam, and you know we have not had any clients in over one month. Our investors and bankers have called, and our notes are due and have started collection proceedings against me and the safari company. They will be coming to repossess all of our vehicles and the passengers' plane. They will pick up all mobile supplies and safari gear, but they cannot touch the lodge or mine and Ladan's home here on this property. I had the deed and contract set up that way to protect you, Wallace and McKenzie, and your farm. We will be losing our home in Dar es Salaam, and we plan on moving here and live in our cottage at least until our child is born. Maybe the war will not last long, and we can get the safari company back up and running."

Wallace said, "I'm sure McKenzie agrees with me, we both would like you and Ladan to live here with us on the farm, and maybe, I can turn you into a farmer."

Lorran said, "I will move part of our furniture from Dar es Salaam to our cottage here before the bank confiscates my freight truck."

Wallace said, "I'm not busy right now, some of the workers and I will help you move, and McKenzie can help Ladan get her home fixed the way she wants to."

Lorran said, "If it's okay, can we head out to Dar es Salaam early in the morning? I don't know when the bankers will be here to pick up the trucks.

The next day, as McKenzie was helping Ladan set up her new home, McKenzie noticed Ladan crying. McKenzie said, "What is wrong?"

Ladan said, "Please don't take this wrong. I love it here at Eden, but I was born and raised in Dar es Salaam, that is my home, and that is where I want to be. Eden is your home, and I feel like I'm infringing on yours and Wallace's home and life."

McKenzie said, "Please don't feel that way, Wallace and I both love you and Lorran like family. We want you here." McKenzie put her arms around Ladan, and they both cried.

Ladan said, "I miss Rowan so much."

McKenzie said, "I do too. I have hardly slept any since he was sent to Belgium." Wallace and Lorran arrived back at Eden after several days near sundown with all of the furniture from the villa in Dar es Salaam. Ladan started crying and went into her bedroom and locked the door and asked Lorran to please not bother her.

McKenzie received a letter from Rowan. He said that he had been wounded but not seriously, just a flesh wound, and he was going to be transported back to England. McKenzie just sat down and caught her breath. She felt so relieved, but she was upset that Rowan had been wounded. She was relieved to know he was on his way back to the safety of England. A week later, McKenzie received a letter from Rowan telling her to tell everyone he was okay. He had been released from the hospital and hoped he could get a pass to come home in several weeks. McKenzie was so excited and ran and told everyone the good news. Several weeks later, McKenzie received another letter from Rowan, and he told her his request had been denied and that his company was training for a mission to go to Burma. McKenzie's heart was broken. She went to find Ladan and told her the news. Ladan wrapped her arms around McKenzie, and they both cried together.

Chapter 17

Plane Crash

Lorran still had his smaller plane; he did not mortgage it to the banks, so he got a job of flying the mail from Dar es Salaam to Arusha, Nairobi, and Moshi. It added a steady income back into Ladan and Lorran's life, and she felt much better about the financial future. A couple of weeks later, Lorran came home and told Ladan that he had met a film producer who wanted him to fly his cameraman over Lake Victoria, Lake Tanganyika, the Serengeti, and the Maasai Mara while he filmed the animals and birds. Lorran said he had agreed to pay him 1,500 pounds sterling, and in two days, they would earn more cash than he could clear in a month carrying the mail. Ladan said, "Will it be dangerous?"

Lorran said, "No, not for me, you know I'm the best pilot in Africa." Ladan had a bad feeling about this flight. She didn't know why; she hardly worried anymore like she used to. Lorran was a very good pilot, and he had never had an accident before. Lorran kissed Ladan goodbye. She said, "Please be careful, I just don't feel good about this trip."

Lorran responded, "If anything does go wrong with the plane, I could sit it down anywhere, no worry. This is no more dangerous than me driving the truck to Arusha."

As Lorran flew out of sight, Ladan walked up to McKenzie's house. She said, "I just don't feel good about Lorran's trip today. I just can't explain it." Two days passed, and no one had heard from Lorran or the cameraman. Wallace, Elias, Kasi, and Kenon drove out into the savanna looking for any signs of Lorran. They drove till they reached Mwanza near Lake Victoria. When they arrived there, a missionary told them that some Maasai men have found a plane crash with two dead White bodies in it, and they had taken the bodies to the constable's office. Wallace asked for directions and when he arrived at the police station. He went in and asked the officer about the two White men's bodies that the Maasai had found. The officer told them the bodies had been taken to the undertaker's office down the street. Wallace asked the officer if he knew what caused the plane to crash. The office said, "The Maasai said the plane had vultures stuck in the cockpit and the engine. He said the plane must have been flying too close to the ground, and the flock of vultures, which were feeding on a dead animal's carcass, were frightened by the plane's low approach and flew up into the plane, causing it to crash." The officer asked if he was kin to the victims. Wallace said no, but the pilot was his best friend. Wallace and Elias drove up to the morgue, went in, and asked to see the two dead White men's bodies. When the mortician pulled back the white sheet covering the bodies, Wallace recognized one of the victims as Lorran, and he asked if he could transport the bodies back to Endulen before the bodies started to decay. The mortician told Wallace that he had done all he could to preserve the bodies. He said they were in pretty good shape when the Maasai brought them in. He said, "We can salt them down, but you probably need to have a closed casket service when you get back to Endulen."

When they reached Eden, Dr. Finley was there. He had flown out to the farm to tell McKenzie and Ladan that two White men had been found in a plane crash near Lake Victoria. Ladan was devastated. She asked McKenzie, "What will I do? I have no man to take care of me, no job, and I will be having a child real soon." McKenzie held her close to her body and told her she was family, and she would treat her as if she was her daughter.

Lorran was buried on the hill next to Dr. Dunn. It was a sad day at Eden. Lorran was loved by everyone. The Hadzabe people had a big feast and ceremony in Lorran's honor. Elias stuck a spear at the foot of Lorran's grave and laid a Maasai shield on top of the grave and said, "Lorran was a hunter and warrior, and he was my friend."

Several months later, Ladan gave birth to a beautiful baby boy. His hair was as black as a raven, and his eyes were as blue as the blue sky. Ladan named him, Ramsey Ladan Abdi. Several weeks later, McKenzie was holding the baby. She was combing his hair and looked into his blue eyes. Ladan said, "McKenzie, you may hate me for this, but I have something to tell you. You may already have an idea."

McKenzie looked at Ladan and smiled. She said, "Rowan," and Ladan said yes.

"The baby belongs to Rowan. The night before he left, we slept together, Lorran was gone to Nairobi, and I felt so alone, and my heart was hurting because I loved Rowan so much, and I knew I might never see him again."

McKenzie said, "I'm not mad at you. I'm glad that we both have a little piece of Rowan here if God forbids him to return to us."

Ladan said, "I have written Rowan and told him Lorran was killed in a plane crash, do you think I need to write to him and tell him he has a son?"

McKenzie said, "I wish you would, it might be the one thing that will bring Rowan back to us."

Ladan said, "Do you think I should tell Wallace?"

McKenzie said, "Yes, I do, but let's tell him together."

In a couple of days, Ladan received a letter from Rowan. He said his company had been shipped to Burma to fight the Japanese. He said:

> It's hell here. The whole country is one big swamp, many of the men have become sick, some of them have developed typhoid and malaria. We have not seen any Japanese, but the diseases and living conditions are terrible. Please keep me and my friends in your thoughts and prayers.
>
> Rowan

Ladan did not receive any more letters from Rowan.

Chapter 18

Missing in Action

Four weeks later, McKenzie and Wallace received a letter from the British Defense Department stating Rowan was missing in action. The letter said that his company had been overrun by a large Japanese force, and Rowan had been taken as a prisoner or killed. They stated that the family would be kept informed on any changing news about Rowan. The commanding officer, who signed the letter, said all of the African soldiers were brave, tough young men and thanked the family for Rowan's service and said, "Don't give up hope."

McKenzie, Wallace, and Ladan were all devastated by the letter. McKenzie said, "I hate England! Why did Rowan have to go, he is my only son. Why do we Africans even have to fight for England?" Ladan went to her room and buried her head into her pillow. She had lost the two men she loved in the last couple of months. "What will I do?" She picked up Ramsey and squeezed and kissed him, at least she had a part of Rowan to hold on to.

Time passed at Eden. Coffee prices were good, and Wallace had another good crop almost ready to harvest. Ramsey was six years old now. He was a beautiful child with dark-olive skin, black hair, and blue eyes. He favored Rowan and had a lot of the same characteristics as Rowan did.

Chapter 19

Communism

World War II was over, and the economy was starting to pick back up, but a wind was blowing in Africa, and it was an evil wind. When Japan and Germany were defeated in World War II, Russia and China seized much of the land and wealth that Japan and Germany had controlled. Russia and China were expanding, and they were spreading their indoctrination of communism throughout the world, and the evil wind was blowing across East Africa.

Elias had brought his youngest son Kiljo to the main house for Ramsey to have a playmate. Kiljo was two years older than Ramsey and was already an experienced bushman and hunter for his age. Ramsey learned from Kiljo and quickly became very comfortable in his African surroundings. Ramsey would spend the whole day in the bush hunting for a small game. There were a lot of wild guinea fowls near the farm. Often, Ramsey would bring two or three of the birds' homes for Lolo, the cook at the main house, to cook for the family dinner.

Emma had gone away to England for a college education. She wanted to be a nurse and come back and set up a clinic on the farm.

Chapter 20

New Son-in-Law

Wallace and McKenzie received a letter from Emma that she had graduated college and would be returning to Eden. She told her parents she would set up a clinic in the old hunting lodge, and she was bringing her boyfriend home with her; she wanted her parents to meet him.

Two weeks later, Wallace drove to Dar es Salaam and picked Emma and her fiancé up. When Wallace met them at the dock, Emma introduced her fiancé to her dad. She said, "This is Richard Bruton, your future son-in-law. Richard, this is my dad Wallace." As they drove to Eden, Wallace questioned Richard. Richard was arrogant and rude. Emma had always been shy and would let other people bully her. She had definitely picked a man who was controlling and critical of her. Wallace was not very impressed with Emma's selection for a future mate.

When they reached Eden, Emma introduced Richard to her mom and Ladan. As Wallace and Richard were unloading the luggage to take in the house, Ramsey and Kiljo came running up; they had been hunting with their bows and had several guinea fowls for dinner. Richard commented toward Ramsey, "That must be one of those little Creamy's Black boys I have heard my friends talk about." He looked at Emma and said, "Is his mommy Black, or is his daddy Black? I'm sure it's his mommy. I have heard how the White men here like to have one or two Black mistresses down here in Africa."

Ladan slapped Richard's face and said, "You disrespectful *sob*. He is my son, and his father was Emma's brother." She turned and grabbed Ramsey's hand and walked toward her cottage. Wallace said, "Richard, you are way out of line. When Ladan simmers down, I want you to apologize to her. Remember, this is my home, and you are a guest here, and you will act like a guest, or I will send your snotty white ass back to England."

Emma ran into the house crying. McKenzie said, "All of you are tired from the long trip, let's all have some food and get some rest. I pray everyone is more civil tomorrow."

Richard went to Emma's room. Wallace heard Richard raising his voice to Emma. He grabbed his rifle, opened the door, and said, "Is everything in here okay?"

Emma and Richard both said, "Yes, sir."

McKenzie took some food to Emma's room and left it at the door and went back to the dining table and sat down with Wallace. She said, "I was not too impressed with my first impression of your new son-in-law. What do you think is his impression of us?"

Wallace said, "When I went to the door with my rifle, I think I had a very positive impression on that young man."

The next morning, everyone was very much more civil, and Richard apologized for his rudeness. He apologized to Ramsey and Ladan. Ladan said she was sorry also. "When it comes to Ramsey, I will protect him with my life."

That night at dinner, Emma asked her mom if she thought that Pastor Sharp would marry her and Richard there on the farm. McKenzie said, "I'm sure that Pastor Sharp would be honored, he has known you since you were a child."

The following Sunday, the whole family drove over to the mission, and after church, Emma asked Pastor Sharp if he would marry her and Richard. He said, "Yes, it would be my honor." He asked her if she had set a date, and she said June 1. He said that's only two weeks away. He chuckled and said, "I will see if I can work that into my busy schedule." The days flew by, and it was the day of the big wedding. The first wedding ever at Eden. Emma, Ladan, and McKenzie had decorated the hunting lodge, and it was beautiful. Emma had asked her dad if he would take her and Richard on a tented safari into the Serengeti. Emma said Richard had always wanted to go on a safari, and she promised him that when they were married, she would get her dad to take them on the safari of his dreams for their honeymoon.

Pastor Sharp performed the ceremony, and Emma and Richard were married. Angel had prepared a big feast and ceremonial dance by the Hadzabe tribe, and everyone celebrated into the night. The next morning, Wallace, Richard, and Emma set out on their safari honeymoon vacation. Wallace drove the couple out to the Serengeti and made camp on a little hill overlooking a small lake where acacia trees dotted the horizon. Wallace set up three tents: one for the dining area, one for him and Kasi, and one for Emma and Richard. Wallace said, "I will give you all the privacy you two need, let me know when you want to dine and if you want to go out on a sightseeing tour." I was your age once, so you won't realize that Kasi and I are here." That night, Wallace prepared a very large romantic candlelit dinner for the young couple, and Kasi prepared a campfire for them where they could sit and be alone near their tent.

The next morning, Richard asked Wallace if he would take him on a lion hunt. He said he had read and dreamed of hunting a large male lion in Africa. Emma begged her dad to please take Richard on a lion hunt. He had dreamed of a lion hunt ever since the first time she had told him that she had grown up in African at a safari camp. Wallace asked Richard if he knew how to fire a gun and if he had ever hunted before. Richard said, "Yes, I'm quite a marksman, and I have hunted and killed a wild boar on my uncle's estate in England."

Wallace said, "Have you ever had a wild boar to charge you?"

Richard said, "Yes, several times." Wallace told Kasi to get the guns ready, we are going on a hunting safari. Kasi jumped high into the air and let out a Maasai war cry.

Wallace, Emma, Richard, and Kasi loaded into the jeep and started across the savanna. Kasi said, "I think I know where a big male has been hanging out," and pointed the direction to Wallace as they drew near to large kopjes. Kasi stopped and jumped out of the jeep and circled the kopjes to the left of the jeep as he reached a large boulder. He stopped and motioned for Wallace and Richard to come forward. Wallace told Emma to stay in the jeep. As Wallace and Richard approached, they saw a large male lion eating a zebra that he had just killed. Wallace told Richard to get ready. He said, "I will back you up if you need help, but I will not fire unless I feel that you are in danger. Aim well, fire, then reload quickly. There may be more lions here, and we may have another charge from a different direction."

Richard said, "I'm ready."

Kasi jumped up and down and yelled. The lion charged. Richard dropped the lion with the first shot. Wallace congratulated Richard. Kasi started skinning the lion. He said, "This will make you and Emma a great rug for your bedroom."

They stayed and hunted for two more days. Richard seemed like a different man. He was very thankful and polite to Emma. Wallace thought to himself, *Maybe I got the wrong impression about Richard when I first met him. Maybe he is a good man and will make Emma a good husband.*

When they returned to Eden, Richard asked Wallace if he could sit down with him sometime and discuss a business proposition.

Wallace said sure. Richard asked Wallace if he would mind if he and Emma started the safari service back up. Richard said, "I have a good friend who would like to partner with me, his family is wealthy, and he would provide all the finances for the operation."

Wallace said, "I don't know, let me discuss it with McKenzie. You know we are getting older, and we like the quiet and peace we have here at the farm."

That night, Emma came up to where Wallace and McKenzie were sitting in the porch swing. She said, "Please, Mom and Dad, you and Dad have the coffee plantation here. Richard and I don't really have anything. You and Dad let Rowan partner with Lorran on the hunting lodge. Please help me and Richard get a start in life, it has been his dream to run a safari lodge for a long time. And, Dad, if Richard is happy, then I am happy, please give us a chance!"

McKenzie looked at Wallace and said, "Let's help them, honey."

Wallace said, "Okay, but before you make any large financial decisions about the lodge, you have to discuss them with your mom and me first."

Emma hugged Wallace and McKenzie and said, "I love you both so much. I've got to tell Richard right now, he will be excited."

Wallace looked at McKenzie and said, "I hope we are doing the right thing. I'm still not 100 percent sure about Richard. I think he is the kind of man who can turn on the charm when it's going to benefit him. I hope he is not using our daughter to get a free safari service at her and our expense."

A week later, Richard's friend, Walt Mahan, flew into the airstrip and had a business meeting with Wallace and Richard. Wallace's impression of him was that of a politician, a man who would promise and tell you everything he thought you wanted to hear.

A couple of weeks later, supplies started rolling into the lodge and the safari camps. Richard had hired three professional guides, and they brought workers in from Nairobi and game trackers from Kenya. The Hadzabe people were not happy, neither was Elias. Wallace told Richard and Emma that the operation had always been family run, and they always let the Hadzabe have a say in the operation of the business. Richard raised his voice, "I'm running it like a business."

Wallace's face turned red, and he stood up and said, "This still is my land, and if you don't show more respect to me and McKenzie and the Hadzabe people, I will close this operation down immediately!"

Emma walked in between Richard and Wallace. She said, "Dad, let me talk to Richard." Richard and Emma walked away a couple of hours later. Richard came back up to the main house and apologized to Wallace and McKenzie. He said, "I'm sorry, I know this is your land, and the lodge belongs to you. I give you my word, I will respect you and McKenzie, and I will send the trackers and workers back to Nairobi, and we will use the Hadzabe people for workers at the lodge and camps."

After the confrontation, things ran more smoothly. Richard was never really friendly with Wallace and McKenzie, and the relationship was more like a business relationship than a family relationship.

The safari business was booming, and guests were shuttled in and out of the airstrip weekly. Elias and his sons, Kasi and Mando, were the main trackers. Sometimes, Elias took Kiljo and Ramsey on less dangerous hunts. One morning, Walt Mahan flew his plane into the small airstrip at the coffee plantation and walked to the main house to visit Wallace and Richard. Ramsey and Kiljo saw Walt's plane sitting on the airstrip unattended. Ramsey and Kiljo had often played like they were flying across the Serengeti in Dr. Finley's and Walt's planes before when they had left the planes unattended on the airstrip. Ramsey and Kiljo ran down to the airstrip and climbed into Walt's plane. Ramsey sat down in the pilot's seat, and Kiljo sat in the passenger's seat. Ramsey started playing with the instrument panel. He turned the ignition switch, and the plane's engine roared to life. The plane started moving down the runway of the airstrip. As the speed of the plane started to increase, it slowly started to rise off the ground. Kiljo cried out, "We're flying!" Ramsey wisely turned the ignition switch off, and the plane glided back to the grassy runway on the landing strip. Both boys jumped out of the plane and ran back to the coffee warehouse. Kiljo said, "We are both real pilots now since we have really flown a plane by ourselves." After Walt located his plane on the far end of the airstrip, both Ramsey and Kiljo were banned from ever playing in his plane unsupervised again.

The coffee plantation was doing well, and Angel was always trying to improve the quality and production of the operation.

Chapter 21

Elephant Revenge

Everything seemed to be going well until one morning, Angel came running up to the house and said that two large elephants were destroying the coffee bushes and the irrigation system. Wallace grabbed his gun and ran toward the coffee field. Elias, Kiljo, and Ramsey caught up with him. Elias had a spear, and Ramsey and Kiljo had their bows. Elias told everyone to stop and stand still. He said, "I know those two large bulls. Do you remember when Riks Becker killed that herd of elephants? Those two bull elephants were the only surviving calves of that herd. They have always hated men since that day. They have torn up several villages that I know of. They have been living north of the farm for several years. I have no idea why they have come here now. They are very dangerous." He told Kiljo and Ramsey to run back to the lodge and get two more large rifles and plenty of shells. Elias told Wallace he didn't want to kill the elephants, but if they charged, they would have to kill them. Ramsey and Kiljo returned with the rifles, and Wallace told the boys to climb up on some large rocks nearby. Wallace took one of the guns and loaded it and laid it on a rock next to him. Elias loaded the other gun and fired into the air; both elephants charged. Wallace fired two times, picked up the other gun, and fired the shot, dropping the big elephant on his left. The other elephant kept charging. Wallace fired again, and he could hear Elias's firing, then he saw the big elephant fall and slid between two rows of coffee bushes. Elias walked up to one of the elephants;

it was still alive. Elias put his hand on the elephants' heads and put his head next to the elephant's eyes. Elias said something to the large beast, then turned and walked to the other elephant and did the same thing. Then, he held his hands to the sky and let out a sad moan and walked back toward Wallace. Wallace could see tears in Elias's eyes; he had not seen him cry since his son was killed by Riks.

Wallace told Ramsey and Kiljo to get Angel and some of the workers. When Angel arrived, Wallace told him to get the workers busy repairing the irrigation system and try to tie up the damaged coffee bushes where they may be able to save them. He told the other workers to get all of the men and women of the village to start preparing the meat from the large elephants. That night, the Hadzabe celebrated and feasted on the fresh elephant meat.

When Richard returned from the safari, he told Wallace that a coffee plantation in Northwest Kenya had been raided by a group of Marxist guerrillas who had raped the White women there and cut the nipples off their breasts. While they made the White men watch, then they slit the White men's throats. Richard was in a panic. "Do we need to get our women out now?"

Wallace said, "I think we are okay. That's the third instance of a raid in North Kenya that I have heard of this year. I don't know of any activity anywhere near here, and I know McKenzie and Ladan would never leave anyway."

Wallace said the new revolutionaries are backed by the communist. Their goal was to run all White men out of Africa, and if they do kill and run them out, they would take over the world that we know as Africa. The Africa that they all loved and cherished would be lost forever. The communist had no respect for the local population and no respect for the wildlife and environment. All they wanted was money and power. Wallace said they are a part of the Mau Mau uprising and the KLFA uprising.

Chapter 22

The Massacre

"I just hope they stay north of us. We have enough problems without having a Marxist revolution."

Everything ran smoothly, and it's quite over twelve months when Wallace got a word of another farm massacre in Northern Tanzania. This raid was only about forty miles north of Eden. A couple of days later, a British captain and his pilot landed at the landing strip. He asked Ramsey and Kiljo if Wallace was at the house, and they told him that he was at the coffee roaster. He asked the boys to show him the way to the roaster; he needed to talk to Wallace. The captain told Wallace that two groups of the Mau Mau had crossed over the border from Kenya and were headed in his direction. The captain said he had two hundred soldiers coming from Dar es Salaam by truck and another 120 soldiers who were following the Mau Mau out of Kenya. He said, "I will send some of the soldiers to stay here until we can capture or kill these raiders." He told Wallace to take extra precautions to protect the farm, and he said, "If you have safari quests out in the Serengeti, I advise getting them back to the farm for their own protection."

Wallace called everyone together and told them what the captain said. Wallace told Emma and Ladan to come and stay at the main house until everything settled down. He radioed Richard and told him to bring all of the guests back to the farm. Wallace issued weapons to all the men at the farm that knew how to use them, and he set up guards around the perimeter of the farm.

Two days later, a truck full of soldiers pulled into the farm; a lieutenant was in charge of the squad of men. He asked to speak to Wallace and McKenzie. He introduced himself as Lieutenant Beasley. He told Wallace that they had just come from the mission at Ngorongoro. He said, "I have some bad news. The missionaries were all killed, and the church was burned. There were one White man and two White women, one middle-aged and a young blond-headed woman. They all had been tortured and burned. We buried them next to the burnt-out church, and we gave them a Christian burial service. I'm afraid that the Mau Mau rebels may be headed this way."

When Richard, Elias, and the rest of the guests arrived back from the safari, Wallace had Richard put them all in the hunting lodge. Wallace posted some of the men around the lodge and asked the lieutenant to send a couple of his men to the lodge to help guard the guests. Wallace asked the lieutenant if he would have a planning session with him. Wallace said, "I was in the military and saw action, and I have lived here in the wild of Africa most of my life. Instead of waiting on the Mau Mau to attack us, let's take the fight to them."

The lieutenant said, "What's your plan?"

Wallace said, "We have the best trackers in Africa right here in this room. They are Elias and his sons, Kasi and Mando. Elias will be able to find the raiders before they find us, and we will take the fight to them."

Lieutenant Beasley said, "That's a plan, they have us outnumbered, and the element of surprise might even the odds." Wallace told Elias to go and try to locate the raiders. Elias took his two sons and ran out of the yard and headed northeast. About four hours later, Kasi returned and said, "We have found the camp." The lieutenant took part of his men and Wallace with Richard and two of his big game hunters, four trackers, and two of the safari guides follow Kasi into the darkness. It took the group about two and a half hours to reach the camp, which was at the bottom of a ravine. Wallace told the lieutenant that he would take his men on the left side of the ravine and for the lieutenant and his men to cover the right side of the ravine. Wallace told the lieutenant, "When I open fire on the Mau Mau rebels, you and your men do the same." Wallace picked out a target and fired. The rest of Wallace's men and soldiers opened up also. The large-caliber elephant guns incinerated the Mau Mau when the bullets struck them. Within minutes, all the Mau Mau lay dead or were dying. Elias and Kasi finished the survivors off with their spears. As Elias killed the last one with his spear, he told the Mau Mau, "This is for what you did to my friends, the missionaries."

It was almost daybreak when the men reached Eden. McKenzie, Ladan, and Emma rewarded them all with a large breakfast with plenty of coffee. The lieutenant told Wallace, "You know, if the word gets back to the Mau Mau leaders of this battle, you and your family will be targeted by them."

Everything settled back down. Richard's Safari business was booming, and Wallace's coffee production was doing well.

Richard started letting Ramsey and Kiljo go on more of the safaris with him and even started letting them train and guide for some of the hunts. Ramsey was fourteen years old, and Kiljo was sixteen. Both of the young men had become very skilled hunters and trackers.

Richard had started drinking more, and sometimes, he would hit or beat one of the African boys for no reason. Richard had always looked down on the Black Africans and did not show any of them any respect, except Elias and Kasi whom he feared because he had seen how brutal they could be to their enemies. Wallace got word of a band of Mau-Mau who had raided a hunting safari in the Maasai Mara and killed the whole party of six White men, two White women, and eight of the African camp staff. He was told that the women had been raped, and all of the victims had been tortured and burned alive. At that time, Richard had three hunting parties in the Serengeti. McKenzie insisted that Wallace would go and find them and warn them of the massacre. When Wallace reached the camp, he found Richard drunk and very belligerent. He told the tracker and the guide at the camp they needed to sober Richard up and move the hunting party back to the lodge. He asked one of the guides where

Ramsey and Kiljo were. He told Wallace that they had taken one of the hunters out that morning and walked off toward the north.

Wallace got in his jeep and headed north. He searched all day for Ramsey and Kiljo but saw no sign of them.

Chapter 23

Richard's Death

Wallace returned to camp late in the afternoon. He found everything in a disarray of sadness and confusion. Ramsey was there but was very upset, and Richard was dead. Wallace grabbed Ramsey and said, "What happened here?"

Ramsey said, "When Kiljo and I took the hunter out this morning, Richard was drunk, and Kiljo took Richard's new rifle. He said Richard was so drunk that we believed he would not realize we had borrowed his gun today. He said Kiljo had wanted to use the new gun ever since Richard had got it, but Richard would not let either one of us touch it. When we returned from the hunt, Richard was waiting on us, and he walked out from behind the big tree and hit Kiljo at the back of the head with a big stick. Kiljo was knocked to the ground and was semiconscious. Richard continued to beat him with the stick with an intention to kill Kiljo. I jumped on Richard's back and began to choke him. He threw me to the ground and started to beat me with the stick. He would have killed me, but Kiljo threw his spear at Richard, and it went all the way through Richard's chest, killing him instantly."

Wallace said, "Where is Kiljo now?"

Ramsey said, "He took his spear and ran off to the north." Wallace asked Ramsey where Elias and Kasi were. Ramsey said, "They are at the mobile camp to the north." Wallace told the camp manager to load Richard's body on the supply truck and take all the staff and guests back to Eden. Wallace said, "Ramsey and I are going to the mobile camp and get Elias and Kasi and try to find Kiljo." When Wallace and Ramsey reached the mobile camp, they found Elias and Kasi celebrating with the hunters they had been guiding. One of the hunters had just killed a large male lion. When Wallace told Elias and Kasi what had happened, Elias went ballistic and struck Wallace, knocking him to the ground. He drew back his spear as if to pin Wallace to the ground with it, then he dropped to his knees and started to moan. He said, "Wallace, two of my sons have been taken from me by White hunters now. I will never guide another hunt for you or any other White hunter." Elias asked Ramsey, "In which direction did Kiljo go?" Ramsey pointed toward the north. Elias told Kasi to go find his brother, and Wallace, Ramsey, and he would follow in the jeep. Kasi took off north at a fast run.

They searched for three days but found no sign of Kiljo or his trail. Elias said, "We will not find Kiljo until he wants to be found, he is a very skilled hunter and tracker. I have trained him well. He will be okay." Elias asked Wallace, "What will happen to Kiljo when we find him?"

Wallace said, "Everyone at the camp saw what happened. Kiljo will have to appear in court, but he has plenty of witnesses to the killing. He killed Richard in self-defense."

Elias said, "It will be a White man's court, Kiljo does not have a chance. He will be hung by the White man."

Chapter 24

Kiljo Is Captured

Kiljo traveled north for four days. He knew if he was captured, the White judge would order him to be hanged. He had seen a man hanged once when he was in Arusha with Ramsey. He was hungry, and his feet were raw from the constant walking. He lay down under a large baobab tree. He was sleeping soundly when some large men grabbed him and put a rope noose around his neck. They tied him to an acacia tree. They started a fire and started roasting a wild pig they had killed. Kiljo had been captured by the Mau Mau guerillas. When his captors had finished eating and drinking, they beat Kiljo. The next morning, they led him to the camp on the Mara River where there were about twenty men and thirty women. They tied Kiljo to a pole in the middle of the camp and let the children harass and throw sticks and cow dung at him. Once a day, a young woman would take him a small bowl of water and some roasted meat. The leader of this band of guerrilla was Amare. One day, he brought Kiljo to his hut; there was a feast of meat and vegetables prepared waiting on Kiljo. Amare had four young women in his hut to service him. Amare asked Kiljo where he was from. Kiljo told Amare he had worked as a guide for a rich safari lodge owner who he had killed in self-defense. Amare asked Kiljo where is this safari lodge located. Kiljo told him it was located west of the Ngorongoro Crater near Endulen. Amare put his arm around Kiljo and said, "Eat, fill yourself with food, then take one of my wives and enjoy yourself tonight."

Kiljo did not know what to think, he had been beaten and abused by the people in this village, now, Amare was treating him like a son or respected guest. Kiljo stuffed himself then took the most beautiful woman in the hut, and they went to the river and bathed. The next morning, Kiljo was awakened by Amare. He said, "You will take me to see this beautiful coffee plantation and safari lodge you have told me about last night."

Kiljo asked Amare, "Why do you want to go to Eden?"

Amare said, "You have described the farm to me so beautifully, I must see it for myself."

Kiljo said, "I think your intentions are to do harm to the people who lived there."

Amare said, "Take me there now or you will die."

Kiljo knew he had done the unthinkable. He had endangered all of his family and friends' lives. He knew if he refused to take the guerrillas, they would kill him, and they could still find the farm. His only option was to go along with Amare's plan and try to slip away from the guerrillas and warn the people of Eden of the Mau Mau raid that was coming.

As the guerrillas started to approach the farm, two of Amare's men grabbed Kiljo and put a rope around his neck, tied his hands, and gagged him.

Luckily, Wallace, McKenzie, Ladan, and Ramsey had gone to the burnt-out mission at Ngorongoro to welcome the new missionaries who were arriving that day. Wallace had sent Angel and a group of workers two weeks earlier to construct a new mission and a new home for the missionaries. Emma had just given birth to a baby son and had decided to stay at Eden that day. Elias and Kasi were at a nearby Maasai village when the Mau Mau attacked the farm and lodge. Part of the Mau Mau herded the cattle and started to drive them back to their camp. The other Mau Mau raiders started killing the men and burning the houses, barns, and coffee warehouses. They set the hunting lodge on fire and raped the Hadzabe women and girls then slit their throats. Two Mau Mau rebels broke into Emma's house, and she shot one of them with one of Richard's guns. The other Mau Mau hacked her to death with a machete. Luckily, she had hidden her baby son behind some boxes in the root cellar, and the raiders did not find him.

Elias and Kasi saw the smoke from the fire, and they started running with ten of their Maasai friends toward the farm. Kiljo freed himself and ran to help save his friends. Just as he arrived at the burning barn, he saw Elias, Kasi, and ten Maasai warriors running toward him. He heard Elias cry out, "How could you do this, Kiljo? I will kill you for this." Kiljo turned and ran into the jungle. Elias, Kasi, and the Maasai quickly killed eight of the Mau Mau; the rest of them fled into the jungle. Kasi asked Elias, "How could Kiljo have done this? Kiljo was always a good boy and loved the farm and the family so much."

Elias let out a vicious scream and said, "I must kill my son Kiljo for what he had done here today."

When Wallace, McKenzie, and the rest of the crew arrived at Eden, they found death and destruction. Elias, Kasi, and the surviving Hadzabe were in mourning. Wallace told Ramsey to go tell Angel, the rest of the workers, and the missionaries to come quickly. He said, "When you have told Angel what has happened, also go to the Rosses' farm and tell him to gather the local farmers and hunters. Tell them to come quickly, we must find the raiders before they kill again."

Chapter 25

Revenge

The next morning, twelve of Wallace's neighbors had shown up to help track the killers. Wallace told Elias and Kasi to track the Mau Mau. He and the other hunters and farmers would follow. Wallace gave Ramsey the gun that Richard was killed over and said, "Your friend Kiljo was part of this raid. I want you to be there when we find him."

Ramsey said, "He was my friend, but I want to be the one to kill him after what he did to Aunt Emma and our farm."

Angel found the baby hidden in the root cellar and brought him to McKenzie. Wallace said, "I hate to leave now, but we must catch and destroy the Mau Mau before they do this to another farm." Wallace told Angel to take charge of the burial of Emma and the dead Hadzabe people. The new missionary, Minister Webb, told Wallace that he and his wife would help Angel in the burial.

Wallace, the farmers, the local hunters, and eight Maasai men followed Kasi and Elias's trail they had left for them to follow. The trail was easy to follow because the Mau Mau were driving the cattle that they had stolen from Eden. That night, Wallace and his men made camp shortly after sunset. Kasi showed up and told Wallace the Mau Mau was heading toward the Mara River to the north. He said Elias was still following them, and he would leave early in the morning and catch back up with his father.

Ramsey was sitting on a rock next to the campfire. Wallace walked over and put his arm around Ramsey and said, "Are you okay, son?"

Ramsey said, "I can't understand how my best friend Kiljo could do this to our family! We were like brothers, and I thought he loved my family."

Wallace said, "I don't understand either, this is totally out of character for Kiljo. There may be more to the story than we know. The Mau Mau may have forced Kiljo to be part of the raid."

Ramsey said, "I would have killed myself before I did what Kiljo did."

The next day after lunch, Wallace and his men came up on a gruesome sight. The Mau Mau had killed about twenty of the cows for no apparent reason and just left them to rot in the sun. Wallace told Ramsey, "We are dealing with some evil perverted men. This is what the Marxist rebels do, they kill the innocent for no reason at all."

"It's just pure evil. I would kill all the Marxist rebels if I could," Ramsey said.

As Wallace and his men were setting up the camp for the night, Elias and Kasi appeared out of the darkness. Elias said, "We have found the Mau Mau camp, it is two miles to the north, they think they have gotten away scot-free. They are butchering the cattle, feasting, and drinking, this will be the time to attack while their bellies are full, and they are sleeping with their women."

Wallace called all of his men around the campfire and drew up a plan for attacking the village, and Wallace asked Elias to lead the men to the village. The Mau Mau have butchered part of the cattle and were roasting the meat on the open fire. The cattle that had not been killed lay on the ground moaning. The Mau Mau had cut the tendons in the cattle's legs so they couldn't run away. Many of the men and women were drunk and passed out around the camp. Wallace estimated there were around twenty Mau Mau men and twenty or more women. He told his men, "We need to send a message to the Mau Mau Marxists. I don't want there to be any survivors! We will show them the same mercy that they showed my family and my people."

He told the men to surround the camp and for everyone to pick a target. Wallace said, "I will fire first," then everyone opened up. "I want no survivors!" Wallace told Kasi and Ramsey to cover the two trails leading out of the camp. "Don't let anyone escape!" Wallace and his men opened fire. The Mau Mau were caught off guard. Kiljo was in Amare's hut tied to a pole. Kiljo knew Wallace had come to inflict his revenge on the Mau Mau. Kiljo grabbed Amare's knife and slit Amare's throat. He then cut the rope off his neck and grabbed the young woman he had slept with several nights before and slipped out of the hut. They ran down the trail that exited the camp. Kiljo almost ran into Ramsey. Kiljo stopped; he and Ramsey just stared at each other for a split second. Ramsey then raised his gun to fire, and Kiljo pushed him down. Ramsey fired at him as he and the young woman ran into the darkness. Ramsey gave chase but soon lost Kiljo's trail.

Back at camp, all of the Mau-Mau men and women were dead or dying. Elias, Kasi, and the Maasai finished the rest of the survivors off with their spears. Ramsey ran back to camp. Wallace said, "Are you okay?"

Ramsey said, "Yes, but I let Kiljo get away. I shot at him, but I missed."

Elias said, "Which way did he go?" and Ramsey pointed to the trail. Elias, Kasi, and the Maasai ran out of the camp after Kiljo.

The next morning, Elias, Kasi, and the Maasai returned to camp. Elias told Wallace that Kiljo had gotten away. He told Wallace that he and Kasi would stay behind at the river and search for Kiljo for several more days and then return to Eden. Elias told Wallace he was sorry for what Kiljo had done. Wallace said to Elias, "I'm sorry too. Kiljo was like a grandson to me."

Wallace, Ramsey, and the rest of the men returned to Eden. When they got home, they visited the grave of Emma.

The men helped Wallace and Ramsey repair the damage of the farm and the hunting lodge. The hunting lodge had not received much fire damage. The main house and guest cottage had some damage, but they were repairable. The coffee warehouse and roasting house had been destroyed almost completely. Wallace's friends told him they would be back next week and help him and Ramsey build the coffee warehouse and roasting house back.

In a couple of days, Elias and Kasi returned. They told Wallace they had followed Kiljo's trail several miles to a large rock formation and lost his trail. Kasi said it was like the earth had just swallowed him up.

The next week, Wallace's friends showed up with lumber and supplies to rebuild the coffee warehouse and roaster house. Within one week, they had the warehouse almost completed. Wallace thanked them and told them he and Ramsey could finish the project. They all gave their condolences for the loss of Emma and the Hadzabe people and thanked Wallace for leading them after the Mau Mau rebels. They said, "If we had not gone after them and wiped them out, they would have come back to our community and killed all of us and our families."

After several weeks, the farm was up and running again. Things were back to a semi-normal lifestyle, but life would never be the same at Eden again after the fire and massacre of the innocence of the precious people who hated no one, loved everybody, and lived their lives in the Eden of Africa.

Ramsey asked Wallace and McKenzie if he could start the safari lodge back and run hunting and photo safaris out of it. Wallace said, "Do you know what you are asking for? Ramsey, you will have no time for the fun things, it will be all work."

Ramsey said, "I grew up helping you and Richard run the safari service. Yes, I know what I'm getting into, and if you say no, I'm going to go to work for a safari service in Arusha."

Wallace said, "Well, if you put it that way, yes, we will help you open the safari service back up, but we are going to keep it on a small scale until you get your feet under yourself and can handle it without me and McKenzie's help."

Within a couple of weeks, Ramsey was taking clients out on hunting and photo safaris. Elias had slowed down a lot and mostly drove the jeep. Kasi was in charge of the trackers, and Ramsey had hired one of his friends from a nearby farm to help him guide, and business was doing well.

Chapter 26

Search for Kiljo

One year later, Ramsey and Kasi were leading a hunting party in the Maasai Mara near the Mara River. Ramsey asked Kasi if he would guide him back to the large rock caves where he and Elias had lost Kiljo's trail after the battle with the Mau Mau. Kasi asked, "Why do you want to go there?"

Ramsey said, "I really don't know why I want to go there, but I have heard some of the hunters working out of Nairobi say they are still some Mau Mau hiding out here near the river."

Kasi said, "If we do find Kiljo, what are we going to do?"

Ramsey said, "I am going to try to trap him and take him back to stand trial."

Kasi said, "You know Kiljo well enough to know he will never surrender. He still remembers seeing that man hanged in Arusha. I remember he could not sleep for weeks after seeing that. It had a traumatic impact on his life."

Ramsey said, "Let's check the big rock formation anyway."

As they approached the rock formation, Ramsey said, "Do you smell that smoke? It smells like someone is roasting meat."

Kasi said, "Yes, I smell it. There is someone up in the rocks." As they got closer, they could tell some people were living nearby the trail to the river, and it was well used. Kasi told Ramsey to get behind that rock. "I hear someone coming! It's a Mau Mau, I can smell him, they all smell the same." As they passed by Kasi, he stepped from behind the rock and slit the throat of the Mau Mau then thrust his spear into the other one. He said, "I hate the Mau Mau for what they did to Kiljo."

Ramsey and Kasi pulled the two bodies into the bush. They followed the trail toward the smell of the smoke. As they reached a clearing next to the rock face of the cliff, they saw a woman cooking meat over the fire. Kasi told Ramsey, "We have just walked right into a Mau Mau camp. I see two more Mau Mau coming up that other trail." Kasi laid his spear down and swung the rifle he was carrying into a firing position. He told Ramsey, "We may have to fight our way out of here. If we get separated, I will meet you back at the river." At that instant, someone fired behind Ramsey and Kasi. The bullet ricocheted off the rock where Ramsey was hiding behind. Ramsey said, "That's not good, they have both trails covered." They saw two of Mau-Mau coming up the trail toward them. The Mau Mau started to run toward Ramsey and Kasi firing their rifles. Ramsey and Kasi fired their weapons at the same time, killing both of the men. The Mau Mau woman ran toward the firepit, picked up one of the dead Mau Mau's rifles, and started firing at Ramsey. Kasi shot her dead; the bullets kept hitting behind Ramsey and Kasi. Ramsey said, "They have got us pinned down, I hope we don't run out of ammo."

All of a sudden, a shot rang out above from the cliff. One of the Mau Mau who was firing from behind Ramsey and Kasi fell dead. The other Mau Mau, who was firing from behind Ramsey and Kasi, darted out from behind the rock where he had been hiding, and the shooter on the cliff above shot him dead. Then, Kasi and Ramsey saw Kiljo standing on the cliff above them. He had shot and killed the two Mau Mau men who had been firing at Kasi and Ramsey from behind them. Kiljo yelled, "Don't shoot me, it's Kiljo!"

He said, "I'm so glad to see you," as he started down the rocky trail to where Ramsey and Kasi were. A shot rang out; another Mau-Mau had come out of the cave entrance and shot Kiljo, and his body came rolling down the rock face. Ramsey took aim and dropped the one remaining Mau Mau rebel. Ramsey and Kasi ran to Kiljo; he was still breathing but was hurt very badly. He said, "I'm glad to see you, my two brothers." He asked, "How is Elias?"

Kasi said, "He is good, he grieves for you all the time."

Kiljo said, "Ramsey, I want you to know I tried to stop the Mau Mau from burning Eden and killing Emma, but they tied and gagged me. Tell father that when I got untied, I was running to stop the Mau Mau from killing Emma, but when I saw Kasi and Dad running toward me, I knew you did not understand, and they would have killed me, so I ran and came here. This was my home, and that woman you shot was my woman. Kasi, I have a young son in the cave, and I want you to promise me that you will take him and love him as your son."

Ramsey took Kiljo's hand and said, "I love you, my brother, and I will see you someday, and we will be together once again in God's Eden." Kiljo's hand slowly slipped out of Ramsey's hand, and he was gone. Ramsey and Kasi reloaded their guns and slowly entered the cave. Kasi saw a small child playing on the floor of the cave. He picked him up and held him high into the air and said, "Let's go home, my son."

Ramsey and Kasi returned to Eden. Elias took his new grandson and held him high in the air and said, "He looks like Kiljo when he was that age." Kasi told the story that Kiljo had told him and

Ramsey about how the Mau Mau had forced Kiljo to come to Eden with them. "They tied him to a tree while they burned and killed the animals, and how he had freed himself and tried to save Emma and how he was afraid that you and Kasi would kill him because we did not know that he was a prisoner of the Mau Mau."

Elias said, "I knew my son Kiljo did not betray me or Wallace's family. I always knew that deep in my heart, and now, my shame has been ratified. My name and honor are restored."

Wallace continued to run the coffee plantation until his health and age caused him to retire. At that time, he turned over the farm to Ramsey, his wife, and son. Ramsey quit running the hunting safari, but he and his son Adam continued to run photo safaris out of Eden.

About the Author

Larry Leslie grew up on the banks of the Tennessee River in the 1950s and 1960s. His early childhood was similar to that of Tom Sawyer. He fished and hunted for whatever treasures the mighty river might bring to the shores of his parents and grandparents' farm along the river. His grandparents had a service station, café, and a bait shop rolled up into one business. They also had the only television set in a twenty-mile square radius of the store. In the late afternoon, men would congregate at the store and order a sandwich and a drink and sit at large wooden tables, watch TV, and tell stories about the war; most of them had just returned from World War II and the Korean War. This is where he learned the art of storytelling. After college, he went to work for a large cooperation where he worked as general manager for forty years. During this time, he was blessed to be able to visit many countries around the world. Larry is an amateur photographer and has a photo gallery. He loves kayaking, snow skiing, and sailing. He is also an avid mountain climber who has been blessed to climb on all seven continents. He just recently retired and started writing; this is something he always wanted to do. *Tears of the African Son's* is his fifth book. He lives on a cattle farm in the northeast of Alabama.

CPSIA information can be obtained
at www.ICGtesting.com
Printed in the USA
BVHW062021011221
622865BV00006B/238